RESILIENT REIGN
ALEATHA ROMIG
NEW YORK TIMES BESTSELLING AUTHOR

Book two of the Royal Reflections Series

Aleatha Romig

New York Times, Wall Street Journal, and USA Today bestselling author

COPYRIGHT AND LICENSE INFORMATION

RESILIENT REIGN

Book 2 of the Royal Reflections series
Copyright @ 2023 Romig Works, LLC
Published by Romig Works, LLC
2023 Edition
ISBN: 978-1-956414-54-7
Cover art: Letitia Hasser at RBADesigns/Romantic Book Affairs
Editing: Lisa Aurello
Formatting: Romig Works, LLC
Proofreader: Stacy Zitano Inman

This is a work of fiction. Names, characters, places, and incidents either are the product of the author's imagination or are used fictitiously, and any resemblance to any actual persons, living or dead, events, or locales is entirely coincidental.

2023 Edition License

Resilient Reign

***"He who does not trust enough, will not be trusted." *** ~ **Lao Tzu**

The halls of Molave Palace and Annabella Castle have secrets that are meant to stay buried. As the reflective veil is ripped away, Princess Lucille is forced to accept the deception surrounding all that she once believed to be true.

To stay resilient in their reign, Princess Lucille and Prince Roman must decide who is trustworthy and who is ruthless, who is friend and who is foe. Even the complicity of family is questioned as the prince and princess fight for their own survival.

Can they even trust one another?

Have you been Aleatha'd?

From New York Times bestselling author Aleatha Romig comes a brand-new contemporary romantic-suspense series, Royal Reflections, set in the world of the royal elite, where things are not as they appear.

*RESILIENT REIGN is book two of the Royal Reflections series that began with RUTHLESS REIGN, followed by RESILIENT REIGN, and continues in RAVISHING REIGN.

Prologue

End of book 1, RUTHLESS REIGN

Oliver

My eyes widened as I took in the words. I could have written the entry before me. The handwriting was familiar. That wasn't what could have made it mine. It was the words. This seemed impossible to comprehend, but as I scanned the page, my gut told me it wasn't impossible. After all, the Firm had found me.

Lucille reached for my arm, her touch cold and trembling.

"Come," I said, "let's take this out into the bedchamber."

"Roman, what does it say?"

I didn't want to tell Lucille what I'd read. Seeing the worry in her blue eyes, I wanted the opposite, to make her happy. However, she'd been the one to say we were in this together. Maybe if Roman, the last Roman, had trusted her, things would have ended differently.

The temperature rose as we returned to the bedchamber. I led Lucille to the bed. "Here," I said, lifting back the blankets. "You're shivering." I saw her bare feet beneath the hem of the nightgown.

It seemed that during each pivotal juncture in our short relationship, Lucille was without shoes.

Doing as I said, Princess Lucille scooted under the covers and continued moving, making room for me. Her blue eyes pleaded, giving impact to her words. "Please sit with me. Whatever this is, I don't want to learn it alone."

I nodded as I kicked off my loafers and slid under the covers still wearing my shirt and pants. Opening the journal, I began reading the handwritten entry.

"If anyone is reading this, I've failed and been replaced."

The words hit me with the impact of a physical punch. I turned to Lucille, wondering what she could possibly be thinking.

"Go on," she said.

"Are you sure?"

She nodded.

I continued reading. *"I haven't decided to chronicle my life to earn your sympathy at my passing. I don't deserve that. I took this assignment. I agreed to take the vow to move from being no one to being someone, to becoming royalty, as if that's even possible. I'm new and still learning.*

"What I didn't realize until it was too late is that ruling Molave is a ruthless task, and King Theodore will continue his ruthless reign no matter who is at his side.

"My real name was Noah Evans. A few days ago and until my last breath, my name was and is Roman Archibald Godfrey. I signed that name and took the place of the crown prince as the heir apparent to the throne of Molave and at the side of Roman's new bride, Lucille Sutton. She isn't to know that I'm not the man she married..."

"Oh my God," Lucille cried, her face falling to her hands. "How is this possible?"

My mind too was scrambling. "There's an entire shelf of journals. Probably a hundred."

Tears flowed from the princess's eyes. "Why? How? Nothing has been real."

Clenching my jaw, I wrapped my arm around Lucille, pulling her quaking body to mine, and vowed to learn the truth. There was one man with the answers, that same man who had replaced his son more than once.

I wasn't sure how, but I'd stay resilient in my new vow. Theodore Godfrey's ruthless reign would end on my watch.

CHAPTER 1

Noah

Five years ago
Journal entry: third day of September

If anyone is reading this, I've failed and been replaced.

I haven't decided to chronicle my life to earn your sympathy at my passing. I don't deserve that. I took this assignment. I agreed to take the vow to move from being no one to being someone, to becoming royalty, as if that's even possible. I'm new and still learning.

What I didn't realize until it was too late is that ruling Molave is a ruthless task, and King Theodore will continue his ruthless reign no matter who is at his side or waiting in the wings.

My real name was Noah Evans. A few days ago, and until my last breath, my name was and will be Roman Archibald Godfrey. I signed that name and took the place of the crown prince as the heir apparent to the throne of Molave and at the side of Roman's new bride, Lucille Sutton. She isn't to know that I'm not the man she married or the man who courted her. I've listened and read. I've been told what to do and what to say, and as I look into the princess's blue eyes, I know it will never be enough.

Seeing her blind trust is infuriating and frightening. I must not let her know that I'm an impostor. Continuing what was begun before me is unfair to the both of us.

I was mad to think that I could do as I'd been asked, to take over another man's life.

For now, my only recourse is in success.

King Theodore is determined to rule past the grave.

Was his true heir unable or unwilling?

I haven't been told.

My charge is to work with the monarch, learn, and take Molave where he is unable to go...past his death.

I've only been at this for a short time, but I understand that my life depends on my success and on the demise of King Theodore.

CHAPTER 2

Lucille

Present time

"Lucille?"

Roman's voice called to me from beyond a fog of confusion. Despite his repeated appeals, I didn't open my eyes or move from the cocoon made up of his bed and the warmth of the blankets. My teeth clenched, my temples ached, and my thoughts spun such as the broken reel of an ancient silent movie. Scenes from splinters of time bombarded my mind.

My first encounter with Roman Godfrey.

The months of study.

His growing discontent.

Had the man I married known of his father's plans? Where is he?

The man who had pretended with me, slept with me, hurt me...

Five years.

"Lucille, look at me."

The deep tenor and resolve shocked my very foundation.

I stayed silent until Roman's large palms held my cheeks, and his firm lips came to mine. Maybe my life was one of a fairy tale. I was the sleeping princess, and this new Roman was my prince charming. His kiss was the key to waking. I pressed against him, needing more of what he could give.

As I opened my eyes, Roman was millimeters away. His thumb gently wiped the tears from my cheeks, ones I hadn't been aware of shedding.

"Nothing is real," I managed to say.

"I'm real. You're real."

"We aren't..."

Sitting against the headboard, Roman pulled me to him and wrapped me in his strong embrace, holding me against his padded chest. Within his arms and the cloud of his cologne, my thoughts began to settle, such as the snow beyond the windows. No longer a blizzard, the flurry lingered as the snowflakes piled one on top of the other, freed from the velocity of the whipping wind.

Time moved, clocks ticked, and the earth continued to spin, yet my only measure of time was the steady beat of Roman's heart. The rhythm was my metronome, lulling my breathing into a steady cadence.

Had I slept?

Was I in a trance?

My scratchy eyes were puffy as I finally peered beyond our cocoon.

When I looked up at the man holding me, his eyes were closed and his breathing consistent. The journal he'd been reading was lying at his other side, opened to pages beyond what he'd read aloud to me.

The clock on the bedside stand alerted me it was after midnight—a new day.

Laying my cheek back on his chest, I wrapped my arms around his torso, overcome with the sadness of what a new day would bring. Today Roman was to return to Molave City. This was the day that I would once again be left alone within the confines of Annabella Castle to face the reflection of my being and what remained of the façade I'd been led to believe was reality.

Beneath my touch, Roman began to stir. His hand moved soothingly on my back in small circles as sleepy reassurances came from his lips. Even in slumber, this man was protecting and encouraging.

What if he were to be replaced?

The alarming new thought pushed away the old.

I sat up and reached out, palming Roman's scruffy cheek. As his long lashes fluttered and his dark orbs focused on me, I said, "You can't fail."

"Princess?"

"The Roman before you—Noah. He said if we read his journal, it meant he had failed and been replaced." My words came faster. "There obviously aren't multiple Roman Godfreys running about. King Theo wouldn't risk that." My pulse quickened. "Do you think he—Noah—is dead?"

Roman swallowed, his Adam's apple bobbing in his throat. "Is it wrong that I wouldn't mourn him?"

I sat back with a gasp.

"His behavior toward you was unforgivable."

"If King Theo would execute him, your life is in jeopardy."

Roman took a deep breath. "I've been trying to think." His dark gaze met mine. "Tell me about Lord Avery."

I shrugged. "He was Roman's equivalent to your Lord Martin."

"And yet I've never met him nor been told about him."

"He knew," I said with a new sense of dread. "Lord Avery knew that Noah wasn't Roman."

"And now he's gone." Roman's dark eyes stared deep into my own. "Princess, you can never let on that you know about me. I knew when I signed Roman's name that I was past the point of no return. Somehow,

I knew. That was my decision. Involving you was wrong."

"King Theo won't replace me." I recalled our conversation in the gazebo and back in the palace. "He asked me to call him Papa in private."

"They're already discussing replacing you, Lucille."

My heart forgot to beat as I heard what was impossible for me to comprehend. Not because I was incapable but because it was too farfetched—more farfetched than the reality facing us. No. Nothing was *too* farfetched.

"What do you mean?" I asked, the conviction in my voice faltering.

"Word of replacing you isn't about creating a lookalike but with us divorcing and me marrying the princess of Borinkia."

"What?" I asked, sitting up, my mind suddenly more aware. "You asked about her this morning. What have you been told?"

Roman took my hands in his. "Lord Martin mentioned that if your procedure isn't successful, there are rumors of a divorce."

"A divorce? Us?"

Indignation filled my words, yet it wasn't righteous. How could it be? I was upset about the end of a marriage that didn't exist.

"From what I can gather," Roman said, "my marriage to Prince Volkov's sister would secure a relationship between Molave and Borinkia."

"Why? The Volkovs invaded Letanonia. Molave doesn't approve of Borinkia. The US doesn't approve."

Roman's forehead furrowed. "You mentioned that your father offered to help you if you chose to divorce."

I nodded.

"And neither he nor your mother ever mentioned that before?"

"No."

"It's too coincidental, Lucille. Your father offers to help you leave, and Lord Martin slips, telling me about a possible divorce and future marriage."

"My father isn't involved in some master plot, Roman. He's concerned about me."

"He knows that as your mother's daughter, there's danger for you in Borinkia. As we've been lying here, I had a new thought."

"Go on."

"I wondered if by removing you from the equation, the Firm believed they'd be helping me stay in character. The Borinkian princess wouldn't know I'm an impostor."

I shook my head. "This doesn't make sense." My gaze met his. "If you, Oliver, were to divorce me as Roman and wed another, would any of it be legal?"

He took a deep breath, his nostrils flaring, and laid his head against the headboard.

"What are you thinking?" I asked.

"I hadn't given it much thought at the time." His gaze met mine. "In my defense, I've had a lot of shit thrown at me in a relatively short time."

"What didn't you think about?"

"It was a conversation with Mrs. Drake."

My lips came together. "Not one of my favorite people."

Roman scoffed. "Princess, that is the first I've heard you disparage anyone."

"I admire her accomplishments. It's that she's as bad as King Theo and....well, you." I smiled. "You know who I mean. She doesn't believe me capable of being more than a shiny accessory."

"I do. I *know* you're more."

"Go on, what were you saying before about her?"

Roman sat taller. "I can't recall my exact question or statement, but I recall her response. She said for me to stop thinking as an American. That here, in Molave, the king makes the rules."

"She wasn't wrong."

"Think about it, Lucille. Noah was right. King Theo is ruthless. There's no other explanation for a man willing to replace his own son with an impostor... more than once." Roman's eyebrows knitted together.

"Was Roman by chance ill around the time of your marriage and honeymoon? Maybe there were concerns regarding that."

I tried to think back. "He was increasingly agitated before the wedding. We had a" —I took a deep breath— "I feel wrong discussing him with you."

Roman brought my knuckles to his lips. "Princess, we must not fail. You hold the knowledge of the previous failures. You're more than an accessory. You are my resilient lifeline and now, as fate has worked its strange reflections, I'm yours."

Nodding, I thought back. "We had a real attraction in the beginning, yet there was always the underlying reality that he was being forced to marry. I suppose I knew that but hoped that there was still attraction and love. After we returned from our honeymoon and he grew increasingly secluded and gruff, I assumed it was because of me."

"How could you have known the reality?"

"I couldn't. Not without being told." My thoughts went back five-plus years.

"Once we were back here, he grew cold, distant, and even..." I didn't finish.

Roman finished the sentence for me. "Mean. Abusive."

I nodded. "Until that point, I'd always been self-assured, yet as my marriage crumbled around me and I was more likely to receive my husband's ire than his affection, I thought all the things I knew were wrong. I blamed myself. I believed if I could be better, he wouldn't..."

"Princess, you know that isn't true. His behavior was his and his alone."

"I provoked." A tear escaped my eye, sliding down my cheek. "I'm ashamed to say that I fell down the rabbit hole that I never imagined. I wanted my prince charming, and he didn't want me."

"It wasn't him."

My chin dropped to my chest. "I know that now."

Roman squeezed my hands. "We must make a decision."

I looked up. "We?"

"We. I won't leave you here in Molave and disappear."

"Disappear?"

"Yes, Princess. Either we both disappear, or we continue this masquerade together. I don't think that either choice is the safe one."

"I-I," I stammered, looking around his bedchamber.

CHAPTER 3

Roman/ Oliver

Lucille's gaze skirted the room, unwilling to meet mine. I wouldn't rush her. The prospects we were both facing were too unlikely and too dangerous to confront with a rash decision. Before I could ask again about what she saw as our future, Lucille's focus landed on the large portrait of a child.

She crossed her arms over her breasts. "I've always wondered why Roman would want that portrait in here."

Turning, I saw the rosy-cheeked child with fair hair wearing a long white dressing gown. "I agree. It's odd to have your own portrait in your bedchamber."

"No," Lucille said, her gaze shifting back to mine. "That's not you. He's your brother."

My eyes widened as I scoured my memory for any information I'd received. There was none. The only sibling I'd been told about was Isabella.

Lucille went on, "He was the king and queen's first

child, born three years before you, and sadly, gone before you were born."

I shook my head. "I wasn't told about him."

"Theodore the third."

"What happened to him?"

"An accident was what I was told. However, I was curious and did further research," she admitted. "He drowned."

"That's awful."

"No one talks about him, yet his portrait is here, and there's one of the king and queen holding him in the gallery around the staircase in the palace in Molave City."

"I assumed that was me," I said with a shrug. "Roman, the real one. How did the young prince drown?"

"The report said that a tragedy hit the royal family. Prince Theodore was found in a pond at Forthwith Castle."

"Where Isabella and Francis live."

"Yes. The castle had been closed after the prince's death. No one went there. The family used this castle as a vacation home after that."

"And now?"

"Forthwith is beautiful. The Firm had it completely renovated for Isabella and Francis. That was during the time you insisted on renovations here."

Her focus went to the still-open passageway before continuing with a sigh. Closing her eyes as if she wasn't ready to continue with the present, Lucille went on about the baby. "I think it's still difficult for the queen and king to visit Forthwith. It's why Rothy's birthday was celebrated at the palace in Molave City."

Cupping her chin, I gently ran my thumb over her cheek. Yes, even after crying, Lucille was beautiful, but as I'd known from the first moment I began studying her, she was so much more. Her blue orbs swirled with different hues. "You have much greater knowledge than I."

"It's taken me nearly six years to accumulate what I know. You've been at this...what? Two months."

"Ten weeks, and you're right. Time is a good teacher."

She turned back to the portrait. "I asked you about him once," she said, "but you wouldn't discuss your brother, saying you were the only heir. Maybe it wasn't Roman...and Noah didn't know..." Her expression paled. "This is all so hard to decipher."

"We need to make a decision, Lucille," I reminded her.

"What will become of Lady Buckingham and Lord Martin?"

"What do you mean?"

"If we would leave, as with Lord Avery...what would become of my mistress and your assistant?"

It wasn't something that I'd thought out. For me, that list would also include Lady Caroline.

Lucille looked down at where our hands were once again connected and back up. "I've never imagined leaving. I took a vow."

"If you ask me, circumstances beyond your control have voided that vow."

Her blue eyes widened. "Circumstances. You mean the king."

"Princess, King Theo knew that Noah wasn't Roman. He knows that I'm not Roman, and still, he perpetuates the fabrication."

She twisted the gold band on my left hand. "I don't want a divorce." Her eyes glistened as she looked up. "I may have hoped for you, wished for you, and prayed for you, but that prayer didn't bring you into being. King Theo and the Firm did that."

My chest ached as I took in her declaration. "You're right again. That's another option." I inhaled and slowly exhaled. "And I believe it is what is best."

"To leave or stay?"

"The divorce is best."

"A divorce?" She shook her head. "No."

"Princess, that option is your ticket to safety. We

divorce and you're out of Molave and away from the king."

"And you'll marry the princess of Borinkia?"

I closed my eyes as I laid my head back on the headboard. "Once you're safe, I'll try to flee."

Lucille shook her head. "He won't allow it."

"Then I too will be replaced."

"By whom? What will become of you? How are there so many people who look like Roman?"

An idea came to mind. "Do you believe that Mrs. Drake, King Theo, Lord Martin, and Lady Caroline are the only people who know the truth?"

"I also know," Lucille said with a shrug of her slender shoulder.

"But you're not supposed to. What about Mr. Davies?"

"I suppose if you were to be examined, he'd notice that your body is" —pink came to her cheeks— "different."

"He did examine me." I tried to recall. "It wasn't long after I arrived. He did a thorough exam. My accent wasn't as good, but he always referred to me as your highness."

"Why do you ask?"

Pushing back the covers, I stood. Still wearing my shirt and pants, I paced near the bed. "I'm the prince. I can tell the royal physician not to do the procedure. If he knows who I am, my dictate won't have the same result. My refusal will probably be shared with the king."

When I looked back at the bed, Lucille had Noah's journal in her lap and her eyes focused down at his writing.

"We should put that back and secure the secret room."

Lifting her gaze to mine, Lucille nodded. "We should. But we also need to read what he wrote—all of it. This will help you. His entries can help you not make the same mistakes." She sat forward. "The conversation with my father. Your dealings may be in these journals."

"And Borinkia," I said, my pulse racing with the prospect of what a treasure trove the journals held. "No. The only mistake would be to stay in this role."

My phone, sitting back on the bedside stand, began to vibrate. The clock near the phone read after one in the morning.

"Who would call this late?" Lucille asked.

I lifted the phone and read the screen. "It's my voice coach."

"I didn't know you had one of those."

Nodding, I hit the green icon as I computed the time in LA. "Dustin. It's late on this side of the pond."

"Oliver...Man, I'm sorry to call at this hour. Truth

is, I hate delivering bad news. I'm not certain what news you're privy to over there and well, you should know."

My thoughts swirled with possibilities.

Something changed with the universe.

They changed their mind and wanted the warlord to return.

No, Andrew would call about that.

"Oliver?"

Perhaps it was hearing my real name, but as I spoke, my accent disappeared. "What news? I haven't heard anything."

Lucille's expression of concern drew me toward her. Sitting on the edge of the bed, I listened to the call.

"It's been all over the news. Andrew crashed his car."

"Andrew Biggs?" My body tensed at the news of my agent. "Tell me that he's okay."

Lucille's hand came to my back with comfort and familiarity that I didn't deserve but welcomed.

"That's just it," Dustin said. "He's not all right. He's gone."

Gone?

I needed to get back to California. "What about his wife?"

"He was alone. There's something that's odd—something I wanted to run by you. You've been with

Andrew for a while," Dustin said. The tone of his voice sent chills over my skin.

"What?"

"The news is saying he had a blood alcohol content of 0.13."

I sat taller. "That's impossible. Andrew doesn't drink alcohol."

"I know."

"Are they suspecting foul play?" I asked.

"No. It just hit me wrong. I wondered what you thought."

"What time did the crash occur?"

"Before noon yesterday. The BAC was just announced before I called you."

My pulse thumped in my temples and my empty stomach twisted.

Could someone have targeted Andrew?

Why?

I said a silent prayer that my gut was wrong. However, in case it wasn't, I lowered my tone and spoke clearly. "Man, erase my number from your phone. Any records or recording of my voice work, delete every fucking second. You don't know me or what has become of me."

"You don't think that Andrew's death could have anything to do with you?"

"I sure as fuck hope not, but the thing is, the Firm

contacted me through Andrew. They knew he was a loose end." My gaze met Lucille's. "I've committed to this role. Things have gotten increasingly dangerous over here. Please don't mention me or where I am to anyone."

"Shit, Oliver, you're freaking me out."

"You were already freaked out. That's why you called."

"I'll delete everything. Tell me," he said, "are you safe?"

I reached for Lucille's hand. "No. But I'm working on it."

"I could call the American Embassy."

"Don't do anything, Dustin. Pretend you never knew me."

With a nod and our goodbyes, I disconnected the call and met Lucille's gaze.

"What happened?" she asked, her blue stare swirling with emotion.

Clearing my throat, I brought my accent back to life. "Recently, the king asked me who knew I was here. Me, Oliver Honeswell. I told him the only one who knew was my agent. I mean, Mrs. Drake contacted him. They would have record."

"What about the man who just called?"

"I never mentioned him."

"And something happened to your agent?" she asked.

"Car crash with a 0.13 level of alcohol." I held tighter to her hand. "Andrew stopped drinking years ago." Taking a deep breath, I asked what I couldn't ask anyone else. "Do you think it's possible that the Firm is responsible?"

Lucille's resolve solidified as she sat taller. "Six weeks ago, I wouldn't have even considered the possibility. I would have said unequivocally no."

"Today?"

"Today, the answer frightens me."

"I don't want you frightened. But we have to face the facts."

"Right now," she said, "I don't want facts. I want you to shed those clothes and climb back into this bed. Then I want to lie in your arms and feel safe until I must go to my own bedchamber."

"Princess, it's not that simple."

"Then make it simple, Your Highness. You are the prince."

CHAPTER 4

Lucille

I feigned sleep as Lady Buckingham entered my bedchamber. I'd been there, alone, for nearly two hours. Thankfully, I'd gotten some sleep in Roman's bed. He'd done as I asked and after securing the journal and hidden room, shed his padded shirt and clothes and joined me wearing his long silk pajama trousers.

Hidden by the dark of his room, I settled beside him, my head on his hard shoulder and my arms around his trim and defined torso. "If the procedure works," I said, "the divorce is off."

"Theoretically," he answered, his arm holding me close before his lips kissed my hair.

"If we flee, we will be found."

Roman's body moved with the nodding of his head.

"What if we stay?" I asked.

"It's too dangerous."

Lifting myself over him, as my vision adapted to the low light, I met his stare through the darkness.

"The answers you need to succeed are in that room. We must continue pretending we know nothing of Noah, and I know nothing of you."

His palm cupped my cheek. "Do you think Roman is being kept somewhere, like *The Man in the Iron Mask*?"

"I can't imagine King Theodore doing that to his son." I lowered my forehead to Roman's bare wide chest and inhaled his scent. The lingering bourbon and cologne, mixed with a unique spiciness, was solely *this* Roman's. "He has to be alive," I said, my words muffled by his skin. I lifted my head. "That's where they'll get the sperm."

I didn't know if I was right—I couldn't fathom another possibility.

The future heir must be blood.

Right?

Roman's command cut through my thoughts. "Refuse."

"The procedure? I would not."

"Refuse anyway."

I inhaled. "May we discuss this at another time, Your Highness?"

Palming my cheeks, his lips met mine. The way our heads turned, aligning our lips, was evidence of our growing familiarity. The twisting of my core and tightening of my nipples were confirmation that my body had accepted Oliver as my husband.

It wasn't only my body.

My heart had accepted the impostor.

Was it wrong?

I hadn't looked for another man.

He'd been given to me.

My thoughts of anything else faded away. Only the present mattered as soft moans came from deep in my throat, and I willingly accepted his tongue. Mine joined the tango as the friction between us sparked our mutual desire. Flames raced across my skin as his touch roamed down my back and behind. My hands ran over his toned torso and up to his broad shoulders. Each indentation and muscle warmed under my touch.

This was the man I'd dreamed of marrying.

One who I desired and made me feel desired.

If only life could be this easy.

As I fell asleep my body tingled with the energy of our union. With dangers lurking around, it was exhaustion that allowed the two of us to settle in each other's embrace.

At the sound of my alarm, I grudgingly eased out of his bed and slipped on my nightgown and dressing gown. With one last glance at the sleeping man, his dark hair mussed, the shadow of scruff on his cheeks, and his firm lips parted, my chest ached with the knowledge of his impending departure. Without a word, I quietly made my way to the other side of our apartments.

After cleaning myself and adding bloomers, I slipped between the cool sheets of my bed. The thoughts I'd pushed away returned with a vengeance.

Where was the real Roman?

How did I not know that the man I married was gone?

Divorce?

My upcoming procedure?

As Lady Buckingham entered my bedchamber and opened the large drapes, I watched with barely parted eyes.

"Your Highness," Lady Buckingham said with a curtsy once the room was filled with natural light.

Pushing myself upward, I sat against the headboard.

Her gaze narrowed as she scanned me from my hair to the blankets. "I've been concerned."

"About?" I inquired.

"The prince. Last night he was...I waited for your call."

"Do not worry. He was agitated about his return to Molave City."

"The physician's orders?"

"The prince is aware of those orders. That too was part of his agitation."

"Are you...well?" she asked. Bowing her head, she looked at me through veiled eyes. "I took the liberty, during the night, to check on you."

Shit.

I worked to keep my expression emotionless. "That was very kind. I'm as well as can be expected." I threw back the blankets, exposing my nightgown, well aware that Lady Buckingham was looking over my exposed skin for evidence that things had not gone peacefully last night.

"I will fetch your clothes for today."

"The prince will be leaving," I said, trying unsuccessfully to stay detached.

"Yes, ma'am. He's currently in his offices. The cars are being made ready."

"His offices? This early?"

"Lord Martin mentioned some business in Molave City, the diplomat banquet, and soon it will be the Fifteen Eurasia Summit. The prince is attending with the king. I will bring you your schedule after your breakfast is delivered."

My schedule.

"I'll be expected for banquet," I said, hoping that I wouldn't be left alone behind the walls of Annabella Castle. The winter weather meant my love of the gardens would no longer sustain me. I could prepare the conservatory for the spring flowers.

"That is up to the prince."

Once Lady Buckingham styled my hair, applied a small amount of makeup to my face, and helped me dress, she made a call to the kitchen and disappeared.

It wasn't long until my breakfast was delivered.

As the maid set the dishes on the small table in the connecting parlor, I was struck with the reality that she had only brought one set of dishes. Roman wouldn't be joining me.

After the maid left, I found myself drawn to Roman's suite within our apartments. My heart beat faster as I knocked on the outer door. With no answer, I twisted the knob and slowly pushed the barrier inward. Holding my breath, I waited for a rebuke.

In all the years of our marriage, I'd never entered his suite without him present. And only recently had I entered without a summons.

"Your Highness," I called.

My voice echoed through the rooms. Step by step, I made my way through the apartment, passing the parlor, the prince's smaller office, a bathroom, his library, and to the entrance of his bedchamber. Biting my lower lip, I turned the knob and entered the same room I'd left much earlier this morning.

The bed was made, leaving no evidence of last night's activities.

Slowly, I turned toward the wall of bookcases.

I knew which case moved, but not how Roman had moved it.

Was there a mechanism?

A switch?

"Princess."

With a gasp, I spun, coming face-to-face with the prince. A scowl replaced the caring expressions of last night. It was then that I noticed Lord Martin, only a few paces behind Roman, still within the hallway. Curtsying, I addressed my husband, "Your Highness."

"What are you doing in here?" His question boomed such as the sounding of an alarm, a perfect improvisation of an aggravated version of his predecessor.

Recognizing his ad-libbing, I lowered my chin and responded appropriately. "I'm sorry, Your Highness. I thought you'd left for Molave City."

"And you came into my suite—my bedchamber?" He turned back to Lord Martin, his voice raised. "Wait for me in the connecting parlor."

"Your Highness," Lord Martin said with a bow.

Roman slammed the door to his bedchamber shut and turned my way. "What are you really doing?" he asked in a much softer tone.

My chest fell as I exhaled.

While my mind and heart were capable of identifying the new Roman, there was still a moment of trepidation when he nailed a believable performance copying his predecessor's demeanor. "I don't know." I looked around. "I was drawn here." I shrugged. "The room. How do I access it?"

"You shouldn't."

I straightened my neck and squared my shoulders. "I should. I will be alone for an indeterminate amount of time." My hands gestured toward the windows. "My garden is unavailable. I have time." My pleas came faster. "I can read and learn and pass what I learn onto you."

"And if you're found with Noah's writings? What then?"

"I've told you," I said, my tenor strong and my volume low. "I'm nothing to the royal family, nothing but a sparkling accessory or a baby maker. I've failed at one, and the man I thought was my husband resented me for the other. My daily schedule will arrive with a full two hours of activities. That leaves twenty-two hours a day for me to fill. I want to fill them with learning more."

Roman's chiseled jaw was rigid, his cheeks freshly shaved, and his brow furrowed. "No. It's too great of a risk."

"A risk of what?"

His strong hands reached for my shoulders. "You, Lucille. I won't risk you. I've decided to approach Mr. Davies and cancel your procedure. If the king questions me, I'll tell him the truth."

"What truth?"

He released his grip. "That I was told about the possibility of divorce, and I support it. The previous Roman—the real one as far as I'd say to the king—made any reunification between the two of us impossible. You hardly speak to me. I'll tell him I insisted on dining alone with you, and the entire experience was horrid. It would be best if I could start over with Inessa."

Inessa.

My mouth grew dry while simultaneously, my eyes moistened at the sound of her name from Roman's lips.

"Inessa?" I questioned too loudly. "That's the princess's name. You know it now." Had he researched her since last night? "You plan to replace me. What does she look like? Is she younger than I? Prettier? Are you truly to discard me so easily?"

In a step, Roman was on me, his one hand in my hair, twisting my long ponytail, and the other on my lower back. His long fingers splayed, pulling my hips and core flush against him as his lips took mine, stealing my words. Unlike our kisses throughout the last few nights, this one was dominating and possessive.

If this were Roman's predecessor, I would be frightened of what was yet to come.

He wasn't.

I wasn't.

This man was the one who throughout the last week had been kind, reassuring, and even protective. This was the man who had brought me pleasure and held me as if I were a precious crown jewel. This wasn't a man to be feared and my body knew it.

As my scalp cried out and his erection pressed against my stomach, mini explosions ignited beneath my skin. From my head to my toes, the energy of his kiss detonated my nerve endings until the only rational thoughts I could process were of him.

When our kiss ended, Roman held my face close to his.

The rumble of his deep tone and measured timbre reverberated through me.

"There has never been a woman I wanted or desired more than you." Pinching my chin, he held my stare. "Inessa is neither beautiful nor ugly. I've spent my life pretending to love women I barely tolerated. I can do that."

I tried to free my chin, but his grip intensified, teetering on painful. "Roman, I don't want you to do that."

"I will because in doing so, I will free you."

"I don't want to be free if it means being without you."

"I've made my decision, Princess. As prince, I have the ability to overrule you."

"Please," I pleaded.

"Live, Princess." He released my chin.

Tears spilled from my eyes as Roman turned toward the door. With his hand on the knob, he straightened his shoulders. With only the view of his back, I heard him speak.

"I'm leaving for Molave City. I'll talk to Papa and report back to you."

"The procedure," I managed to say, wondering why I'd want to have a baby made with the sperm of a man I no longer knew, and also understanding that without that procedure, I would be leaving Molave.

"I will cancel it." He didn't turn to face me. "Goodbye, Lucille."

I stood motionless as Roman walked away, leaving me in his bedchamber all alone.

Slowly, I moved to a large set of windows that looked out on the surrounding property. Gray skies covered the blanketed landscape. The frigid and gloomy view fit perfectly with my onset of emotions.

"Your Highness."

With tears sliding down my cheeks, I turned to my mistress.

"Lucille?" she questioned as she came closer and gently reached for my chin. "I will get you an ice pack."

I shook my head. "I'll have my tea."

"Your breakfast is waiting."

Inhaling, I wiped my cheeks and turned to Lady Buckingham. "It's over, Mary. I tried."

My mistress stepped closer, and in a rare display of affection, she opened her arms.

Without reservation, I stepped to her, leaning my cheek against her shoulder as tears for what was never meant to be bubbled into ugly sobs. I didn't explain what I was feeling because I couldn't.

If I tried the explanation would come out as babble —insane, incoherent, and unbelievable. If I were to explain, I'd have to tell my mistress that I'd finally found the man I could love and support without question. To say the man was my husband, but not. That man reminded me what it was like to be adored. And in a quest to save me, he'd broken me.

CHAPTER 5

Roman/ Oliver

Lord Martin sat at my side as our vehicle within the small caravan of royal-fleet cars progressed south through the Monovia region. It wasn't necessary to tell my assistant that I wasn't in a mood to talk. Some things about Roman Godfrey were becoming second nature, such as exemplifying my foul disposition.

Even with the overcast skies, I had a better view of the mountainous landscape. With each hairpin turn in the road and steep drop-off, I had a better understanding of Lucille's anxiety regarding our trip to Annabella. If I'd been better acquainted with the topography of the land, I would have never risked our lives during the heavy snowfall.

With my expression stern, I watched beyond the windows while my thoughts went back to finding Lucille in my bedchamber. To finding her and to leaving her. I wasn't an empath, yet I'd grown sensitive to her moods and knew what my decision had done to her.

The choice to divorce wasn't an easy one to make. No matter how many times I told myself this was an acting job, I knew that I was lying. Or perhaps only misleading.

Yes, I'd been hired to play a role.

There was a fortune accumulating in an offshore account for when the job was complete.

None of it mattered.

Noah's writings confirmed that the role of Roman Godfrey would be my last.

I'd never see that accumulating wealth.

Any thoughts of retiring with the crown's money and keeping Lucille Sutton at my side were ludicrous. I'd signed my vow knowing the finality of my decision. The same couldn't be said for Lucille. She'd married in good faith, adamantly denying that she was coerced into the agreement.

"Your Highness," Lord Martin said, looking up from the screen of his tablet. "Are you ready to discuss your schedule?"

Sighing, I turned to my assistant. "Go on."

"King Theodore requests your presence upon arrival. Lord Taylor will be in your offices at two to discuss the upcoming summit. Mrs. Drake has requested a meeting.

At this time, she can be fit in at four. There is also the matter of other personal requests from visiting diplomats as well as members of parliament. Tomorrow you will join the king in a meeting with the prime minister."

My jaw ached as I clenched my teeth.

By nature, I wasn't an easily agitated man. In my profession, that of acting, there was a thin line between revered and loathed. One was not to appear too entitled yet also not a pushover. With each success, the line became thinner. "Act like you deserve the success." "Don't alienate your costars." "The Actors Guild will only support you if you support them."

There was never a lack of advice.

In this new role, new life, for over ten weeks I'd been encouraged to recognize the entitlement that came with my position. Even King Theo admonished me for being too accommodating.

"I will see the king," I said, answering Lord Martin while measuring my words. "Lord Taylor will need to be rescheduled for tomorrow. I want Mr. Davies added to my schedule for this afternoon. He will come to my offices."

"Are you ill?" Lord Martin asked.

"Your concern is noted. I'm not ill."

"The royal physician..."

"Will come to me this afternoon. Is there any need for me to be clearer?"

"No, Your Highness."

Silence enveloped the inside of the sedan, yet I'd grown accustomed enough with my assistant to know he was waiting for an opening to voice some opinion. Unlike when this all began, I didn't want his opinion. I didn't want to think about Lucille's question regarding the future of Lord Martin, Lady Caroline, and Lady Buckingham.

I was doing what was best for everyone. When the divorce was finalized, I assumed Lady Buckingham would be reassigned, perhaps to Inessa Volkov. Even thinking her name made my gut tighten and the small hairs at the back of my neck stand to attention.

I'd looked up her image. The description I'd given of neither beautiful nor ugly was accurate. Unlike Lucille's coloring, Inessa's hair was blond, and her eyes were green. She was younger than me, even the real me, at twenty-nine. That made her nine years younger than her brother, the prince of Borinkia and four years younger than Lucille—prime age for childbirth.

In reality, there was no comparison between the two princesses. From the moment I'd caught Lucille's blue gaze in the dining room before Rothy's celebration, the princess of Molave had my heart in her hands. I couldn't define what could or did incite that extreme emotion in a bachelor of thirty-eight years of age. Heaven knows the tabloids had tried to marry me off to a long list of Hollywood stars. They were all women of untold—and mostly unnatural—beauty and varying degrees of talent.

Rita Smalls had been the most recent target. She was also the only name that would appear again and again on the list of possible 'Honeswell heartthrobs.' It wasn't only the thought of Rita with the slime-bag Ronald Estes that left a sour taste in my mouth. It was the memory of her explaining our non-exclusivity combined with my learning of the warlord's demise.

In all the years of our varying relationship, I had never used the *L* word. Okay, some words that begin with *L*, but never *love*. When a reporter would ask Rita and me if we were in love, we would smile at one another and laugh off the question. When pressured, I'd admit to caring for her or having a long relationship that transcended peaks and valleys in our careers.

I wished Rita well with her life choices.

Lucille Sutton was different on every plane.

Never had anyone's presence affected me so deeply.

In the span of six weeks, I'd fallen for the princess.

That was why I would talk to the king about the divorce.

In this strange world, the only way to ensure Lucille's safety was to get her back to the States, back to her parents, and away from the ruthless reign that was infiltrating every minute of our days, weeks, and years.

"Mrs. Drake, Your Highness?"

"Schedule the physician and if time is available, I'll see Mrs. Drake. If not, she too may wait for tomorrow." I debated about broaching the subject of Andrew. If I did, I couldn't tell her how I learned about his death. Then again, Dustin said the information was on the news.

"The queen has requested your presence at dinner."

"Yes, of course." It went without saying that it was odd to be faced with a mother who lacked enough familiarity with her son to differentiate him from an impostor. Losing my mother in my mid-twenties left a void I'd only examined for character development. She died too young of lung cancer.

Ambulance chasers wanted my siblings and me to pursue a legal battle due to our mother's years in the air force. While each of us could've used the money, not one of us was up for the fight.

We gave her the funeral she deserved, split what little remained of her estate, and went our separate ways. I almost chuckled aloud at the idea of contacting one of them and informing them I was now the Prince of Molave. Not only wouldn't I risk their safety, I had no means of contacting them.

Obviously, we weren't close.

I was the oldest by four years.

My two sisters were united by the same father. Our mother wasn't a bad mother. The US Air Force filled her life with travel, which in turn meant upheaval in our lives. In a way, I could thank her for where I was today. My vocal skills and ability to mimic accents was all due to my colorful and well-traveled childhood.

The scenes beyond the windows pulled me from my thoughts. No longer a foreign world, the buildings and city were now familiar.

We'd left the province of Monovia, traveled through the province of Boutch, and were entering Molave City limits. The snow from the mountain regions was nowhere to be seen. This area had only received a cool rain. And today, even the sky was blue this far south.

"Mr. Davies?" I asked.

"Yes, sir. He will be to your offices by half past three."

I looked at my watch. It was only after eleven. "Depending how long I'm with the king, tell Lord Taylor to stand by."

"And Mrs. Drake?"

"I want to see her." And ask her about Andrew— maybe. "Make it work, while giving me enough time to prepare for the late meal."

"Yes, Your Highness."

People beyond the windows waved as the car slowed near the palace gates. Lifting my hand in a stately wave, I nodded, careful to keep my expression subdued. The revered waves and greetings were much different than Oliver would receive on the red carpet of a premiere or awards ceremony. Still, I wasn't unaccustomed to the attention.

That made the indifference easier to display.

Even with the blue skies, the air temperature had dropped, chilling my face and hands as I stepped from the vehicle. Lady Caroline was waiting along with various other palace staff. Bows and curtsies as well as greetings met me as I made my way into the palace.

Lady Caroline was to one side of me, and Lord Martin was on the other.

"Your Highness," Lady Caroline said. "If I may, before your meeting with the king."

Slowing my steps, I led our trio into one of the numerous drawing rooms and closed the door.

"You look well, sir," she said.

My gaze moved from her to Lord Taylor and back. "On with it."

"The princess," she said, "is on her way to Molave Palace."

"What?"

"Yes, Your Highness. After you left Annabella,

King Theodore decided the forecast for the next week was too unpredictable. He ordered Princess Lucille here to Molave City. Her presence is needed for banquet and also, so she won't miss her procedure."

My nostrils flared as I exhaled. "My wife should take orders only from me."

Lady Caroline bobbed her head. "We are all subjects of the king." When I didn't reply, she added, "I apologize, sir. I thought it was best if you were informed before your meeting with his majesty."

"Well, fuck," I muttered.

"Your Highness," Lord Martin admonished.

"Surely," I said in a whisper, "Roman swore."

"He did, sir."

"Is the king ready for me?" I asked both of my assistants.

"Yes, sir. He's been ready since yesterday," Lord Martin replied.

Tugging the cuffs of my suit coat, I rolled my neck from side to side. "Then let's get this over with."

CHAPTER 6

Lucille

With my mistress at my side, we rode the two hours to Molave City in silence. My thoughts were stirred, and my emotions scattered like particles in a cyclone. The tears I'd shed in Roman's bedchamber were dried, my makeup reapplied, and my mask in place.

As our cars neared the southern capital, the gray sky began to break, offering fractured glimpses of light blue. And yet my emotions were far from brightening.

It wasn't long after Roman left Annabella that I received the call. Instead of speaking to one of his advisors, King Theo called me himself. He advised due to the prediction of incoming inclement weather, I should immediately head to Molave City. With the forecast of another heavy snow in the elevations, he didn't want me unable to travel to the palace for the upcoming state banquet. As a side note, he mentioned my appointment with the royal physician.

Speaking to the king on the phone was different

than it had been in the past. I felt a shift within me. No longer was I enamored with the attention of the king. The veil hiding the truth of the monarch had been shredded by the sharp words in Noah's journal. Despite my survival and that of Oliver's hinging upon my ability to appear unchanged, everything had changed.

Hearing King Theo's voice reminded me that this was the man who believed himself sovereign in all things—not only the ruling of Molave, but every aspect of royal life. He believed himself capable of dictating my chances of conception while also offering me as a perk to whatever man he put into Roman's life.

While I didn't and couldn't let on that I knew the hidden ruthless side of King Theo, the man who in the past had only shown me kindness, my tight grip of my phone was an outward sign that something had changed.

I would need to do better in Molave City.

Throughout the drive, I worried that I wouldn't do better. My new prince had awoken a piece of me that I'd allowed to fade into dormancy. In the presence of the king and queen, I would need to aid its slumber.

As Lady Buckingham oversaw the maids packing my things for our trip, I slipped into my private study and sought the knowledge that I hadn't in six weeks. During that time, I hadn't had the means. Now I did.

The bombshell came last night, following the prince's call with a man named Dustin. Roman confided his full name. I wasn't certain that he intended to offer me his last name, but now that I had it, I needed to learn—who was Oliver Honeswell?

The circle swirled upon the screen of my laptop as I waited.

Would this information too be shielded from me?

My eyes opened wide in shock at the description at the top of the page: American actor. And then in picture after picture, I saw his likeness. I was struck with the absurdity: the Firm literally hired an actor. Oliver's list of accomplishments went on for pages. His most recent endeavor was that of playing a warlord in a popular futuristic comic franchise.

Had anyone ever noticed the similarities between the warlord and the Prince of Molave?

Simply thinking the question made me smirk.

As I searched through his information, I learned that not only had Oliver done well in film, but he also had a successful career on Broadway. That knowledge triggered a reminder of some things he'd said over the last six weeks. His declaration played on repeat in my thoughts. He'd said he'd spent his life pretending to love women he barely tolerated. He'd also mentioned a voice coach as well as his agent, the one who was now deceased.

I'd asked him once if he was an actor, and he'd replied that we all were.

The answer was affirmative—Oliver Honeswell was an actor, currently playing the role of Roman Archibald Godfrey, Prince of Molave, Duke of Monovia.

Why did this new knowledge give me hope?

Roman left me in tears with talk of divorce and of Inessa Volkov. The wobbly tower of our marriage that I'd pieced together since the day Oliver appeared in my parlor splintered with tornado-force winds at the declaration of his new decision. As Roman spoke, I'd believed every word as I had since our first meeting.

Why?

The man was good. He was convincing.

He was an actor.

Even with my knowledge of his true identity, there were times throughout the last six weeks when I'd swear he was his predecessor. As often happens with the accumulation of more information, new questions came to mind.

What would make a man give up a successful career to step into the shoes of a total stranger, in a foreign country, where fiction becomes reality, and reality becomes a reflection?

"Your Highness?" Lady Buckingham's voice pulled me from my thoughts and questions.

I turned her way, focusing on her hazel stare, in lieu of a verbal acknowledgment.

"Lord Martin messaged. The prince...he knows you're on your way."

After the way Roman walked away, I hadn't had the nerve to call him myself.

That behavior was more in line with what I would have done before the new Roman.

With my expression unchanged, I nodded and turned back to the window. My thoughts went to the upcoming state banquet. I wondered if I would be able to hold it together on the arm of a man who wanted me gone.

Seeing the sights outside the limits of Molave City, I tried to take my mind off the prince. Our caravan was traveling through a small village in the Boutch province called Brynad. As we approached the main thoroughfare, a growing scene outside the car caught my attention.

"What's happening?" I asked anyone within the car.

Beyond the windows, a crowd of people stood on the walkway in front of a grocer's. With the chilled temperatures, they were wearing warm coats and huddling near one another.

"We should continue on, Your Highness," the guard seated beside the driver said.

"No, wait."

As the driver radioed to the other cars, the slowing of our procession was noticed by the people in the crowd. With the royal crest on our doors, it wouldn't be difficult for them to guess who we were. The only question was which one of the royal family was inside.

Lady Buckingham reached over, laying her hand on mine. "Lucille, remember the last time."

I did.

The new Roman hadn't admonished me, but applauded, saying I was loved and listened to by the people.

"I thought the food shortages were under control," I said in lieu of a reply.

"We should keep moving," the guard said again.

"No." I turned toward Lady Buckingham. "I'm going to speak to them."

Her lips pressed together in a straight line as her complexion paled.

"Radio the other cars," I demanded as the car we were traveling in came to a stop.

As I buttoned my wool coat and slid my hands into long gloves, preparing to meet the people, I had a strange and overpowering sense that this was why I'd agreed to marry Roman, to become princess. It was to help the people, not to live in a remote castle atop a mountain. Roman had mentioned skywriting or banners—something to tell the world about our union.

This, beyond the window, was just that—a proclamation. Not of our union, but of my emerging role. I'd seize it before I could be replaced.

At some point in the last few hours, I was hit with the realization that the Firm would trust the future of Molave to an actor but not to their princess. If my new husband was correct and the people did care for me, then I would be a face and a presence beyond the walls of Annabella Castle. If this worked, it would be more difficult for Roman and the Firm to send me away.

With the guard now outside the car prepared to open the door, I recognized that I was working against Roman's—*this* Roman's—wishes. So be it. I'd spent too long following the rules only to be discarded for another.

Speaking to and for the people could be one of my last chances to fulfill the destiny I'd accepted. Breaking rules wasn't going to stop me.

"Princess Lucille," the crowd chanted as women curtsied and men bowed their heads.

"Please tell me," I said, my voice raised and coming forward in puffs of foggy air, "what is happening?"

There was a nervous murmur before an elderly gentleman stepped forward. "Princess, the market has been closed for three days. There was a rumor of it reopening today. With shelves low of supplies, we didn't want to miss the opportunity."

I looked up and down the street. "Is there another market?"

"No, Your Highness, not without traveling miles."

A woman by his side spoke up. "Those with automobiles tell us that the shops in Deca and Gekfjord are also closed."

"Surely, the grocer has informed you of the reason and given you a time when it will reopen," I said.

The crowd parted, showing me a sign written in both English and Norwegian that said '*Closed until further notice.*'

A younger woman came forward with a curtsy. "Your Highness, those of us who work for the mines were recently paid our wages." She took a deep breath. "My child needs food."

"Three days?" I asked.

The crowd nodded.

"Where is the grocer?"

"Hiding," someone from the crowd yelled.

"Who owns the market?" I asked.

"You do," another woman spoke. "The royal family."

My years of training came back to me. "The stores are to be subsidized if needed, but the ownership is private."

The most recent woman spoke again. "Not anymore."

"When did this change?"

"Are you really so unaware?" the woman said.

I straightened my shoulders as my cheeks continued to chill in the autumn air. "I'm sorry. I am. I'm also on my way to the palace where I'll bring this up with my husband and the king."

While the younger woman didn't appear appeased, the older man who spoke first bowed and offered his thanks. "Thank you, Princess."

Knowing that I was speaking without permission, I added, "I will give you my word to return here tomorrow at this time to ensure that the market is open."

The offers of thankfulness filled the air.

Once I was back in the vehicle with Lady Buckingham, our driver, and a guard, I felt my lips curl into the first smile I'd had since Roman's promise of divorce.

"What you did..." Lady Buckingham said disapprovingly.

"Mary," I said, addressing her by her first name, "if my husband thinks I'm so easily discarded, then I have nothing to lose by vowing to help the citizens of Molave."

"The king."

"Will be angry as will the prince." I laid my gloved

hand on top of her hand. "I'm tired of being an accessory. I'm not leaving Roman or Molave without a fight."

"Where is this coming from?" she asked softly.

Taking a deep breath as the car began to move, I contemplated her question. "It's always been here. I tried playing by the rules, and it's gotten me no place." With my neck straightened and my resolve strengthened, I added, "Now I will fight with what I have as long as I have it."

My title.

My popularity.

CHAPTER 7

Roman

"Your Grace," I said with a bow as I entered King Theodore's private office.

He was seated behind his ornate large desk. Despite the earlier circulated concerns regarding the monarch's health, King Theodore appeared as strong as he had on films I'd viewed from over a year ago. That wasn't to say he hadn't aged. With my studying, I saw how over the years his dark hair turned to white, the wrinkles surrounding his eyes and lips had grown more pronounced, and his body no longer appeared to have the muscles and bulk of a younger man. Even so, there was nothing frail about the monarch before me.

"You were expected yesterday with Lord Taylor." His voice boomed with displeasure, echoing in the large room.

"We communicated yesterday."

"Not in person," he said, standing behind his large desk. "You have responsibilities to the crown and much more to learn. Spending dinners with the princess isn't the best use of your time."

His statement indicated that someone among Lucille's and my staff reported to the king. I'd have to give that more thought another time. Now, my focus was on King Theodore and the inroad he'd unwittingly offered. "I fear, sir, that any ongoing relationship between the princess and Roman is unlikely. The strain already present is too much."

"Don't speak of him in third person."

"Yes, sir. *Our* relationship is irreparable."

"What has she said?"

"Nothing." I exhaled. "Lucille responds in short sentences as if she can barely tolerate being in the same room with me." If the king was aware of our nightly rendezvous, he'd know I was lying.

King Theo gripped the back of his office chair and shook his head. "It may be too late. My damn son…"

"Sir, I was made aware of a possible answer to this dilemma."

The king's dark eyes snapped to mine. "What answer?"

"Divorce."

"Impossible," he bellowed. "Not as long as the arrangement with Senator Sutton is under negotiation."

"We reached an agreement."

King Theo shook his head. "A gentleman's agreement is far from the final word. Once the new provisions are passed into law, then we can discuss alternatives."

"Inessa Volkov?"

"The States will not agree to work with us if we collaborate with Borinkia. You should know that."

"I do, sir. I also have been made aware that there has already been collaboration."

His eyes narrowed. "By whom?"

"The information was noted among the volumes I've been allowed to access." That wasn't true, but my suspicion that I was onto something facilitated the untruth.

"That is unlikely."

Since I hadn't been offered a seat, I was still standing near the chairs neatly facing the king's desk. I took a step closer. "Your Grace, I have no other way to obtain information. I could look for the document if you'd like to see it." When he didn't speak, I added, "If I'm asked about that possibility at the state banquet or the summit and I respond without the knowledge Roman had, there will be questions."

"No one would dare ask such a question. It's treasonous. The diplomat banquet will be a fine dress rehearsal for dealing with many dignitaries at once."

Lord Martin and Lady Caroline had been

instructing me on behavior during both upcoming events. That didn't mean I was confident.

He spoke about the different ambassadors who would be in attendance.

I wasn't as easily distracted. "Back to what I'd been told. Are you informing me that officially there has been no talk of the princess and me divorcing or a union between the princess of Borinkia and myself?"

His dark stare studied me up and down. "Persistent. That can be a good quality when not used with me."

"It is my vow to support Molave, not to cause harm because I didn't properly prepare."

The king took a deep breath. "An arrangement such as that could make your life—your role—easier. You wouldn't have the concern of Princess Lucille."

What the hell?

Now he was admitting such a discussion.

"If that is the plan, I'll keep it close to my vest." I took a deep breath. "There's no reason for Lucille to complete the procedure. It wouldn't make sense for her to become pregnant and then divorce."

"The procedure is set. Lucille is on her way to Molave City." He exhaled. "You should have insisted she accompany you since the banquet is a few nights away."

"You've told me to have little interaction."

"A different car."

I gestured toward the chair. "May I?"

The king nodded as he took his seat again. Leaning forward, he placed his hands on the top of the desk. "As a small sovereign country, we must constantly be on watch. Lucille is our ace in the hole, so to speak, when it comes to the States. Getting on the bad side of her country won't help Molave."

"Why negotiate with Borinkia at all?"

"It was Roman's idea," King Theodore said, exhaling and sitting back against the chair. "Merging Borinkia and Molave would more than double our landmass. The additional port cities would help with trade. Borinkia has been hit with embargoes since overtaking Letanonia. Time heals all. It's been nearly two decades, and Borinkia wants to be recognized as part of the European Union and as an ally around the world."

"Prince Volkov rules Borinkia," I said, knowing that was true. "I'm less familiar with its government. Does he answer to a parliament or advisors?"

"Yes and no."

"Basically, he's similar to your role."

"Yes," the king replied. "Absolute power."

"Did Roman tell you he was working with Alek?"

The king's jaw clenched. "This subject is classified above your clearance."

"How did you find out?"

I knew I was pushing, but I had the feeling I was onto something big. Maybe Noah's downfall.

"I'd heard rumors. I confronted him. He lied to me."

"Is that the reason," I asked, "why I'm here?"

One nod.

Almost imperceptible.

It was my answer.

"Do you want me to continue covert communications with Alek, or do you want that line of communication to disappear?"

"I want both, the US and Borinkia. I want more than that, but Borinkia could make Molave a greater power."

"Wouldn't it work both ways?" When the king merely appeared puzzled, I went on, "Molave could make Borinkia a greater power. Molave has more allies and a higher standing across world leaders."

The king nodded. "That was Roman's mistake. While he only saw Molave as the victor, the negotiations he was facilitating could too easily have resulted in Molave's defeat. Right now, we can't risk our relationship with the US. Once Lucille's procedure is complete, you have my permission to work on improving your marriage."

It took every ounce of determination to keep my lips from moving, from telling King Theodore how archaic and misogynistic it was for him to grant permission to those who weren't his to give.

"Sir? She's married to your son."

"You are now he."

"Surely, when Roman returns..."

"I will speak to Elizabeth about increasing your salary."

My salary?

Was I now being paid to fuck the princess, to keep her happy?

"My salary is sufficient, Your Majesty. Maintaining a relationship with the princess was not in the job description."

"Yet you're willing to consummate a marriage with Inessa?"

"No. Yes. It would be *my* marriage."

"If it will ease your mind, I'll have the Senior Cardinal Decoti from the Church of Molave visit you under the pretext of blessing the reunification of your marriage to Lucille. It's a common procedure when there has been discord."

I found myself at a loss for words, an unusual situation for a man in my profession—however, labeling my new profession was becoming more difficult.

Prince.

Duke.

Son.

Husband.

Prostitute.

Before I could respond, the sound of voices grew louder beyond the king's door leading to the outer offices. His dark gaze turned to me questioningly. I stood, standing between the door and the king. It wasn't a thought-out decision but rather an instinctive sense of duty I felt to a man who didn't deserve it.

Add bodyguard to my job description.

One of the double doors opened inward.

"Your Majesty, Your Highness," the young royal guard said with a bow. "Princess Lucille is here to see you."

"I didn't send for her," King Theodore said. "Tell her to return when I call."

Lucille appeared behind the guard. "Your Grace," she said with a curtsy. Her eyes only on the king.

"Lucille, what is the meaning of this?" the king questioned.

My pulse quickened with her presence. There was a new quality in her beautiful blue stare, in her straight posture, and in the way she presented herself.

She lifted her chin. "You sent for me, demanding my presence. I'm now here for an audience with my king."

CHAPTER 8

Lucille

Silence hung heavily in the air. With each passing second, my mouth grew dryer and my skin prickled. Maintaining my façade, I kept my attention on King Theo as everyone awaited his response. That wasn't to say I was unaffected by the presence of my husband. I felt his stare, not with the dread as before, yet his presence was palpable. There was no way I could meet his gaze and keep my nerve.

With a nod and exhale, King Theo gestured for the guard to allow me entry.

"I will leave the two of you, Papa," Roman volunteered.

The door closed behind me.

I took a step forward and again offered King Theo a curtsy. "Thank you, Your Grace."

The king motioned toward the chairs facing his desk. "Sit, *both* of you."

"Your Highness," I said, my gaze barely meeting Roman's.

While I'd only walked a few steps, it felt as if I'd finished a marathon. Once we were all seated, I tried to control the racing pace of my heart.

"Lucille," the king said, his dark stare on me. "It's good to see that you're well from your trip. You and Roman will be expected to take part in the upcoming state banquet."

"Yes," I replied but wanting to move beyond pageantry.

"The royal jeweler will be at your disposal for whatever you choose to wear."

A shiny accessory.

Taking a deep breath, I resolved that there would be more to me than gowns and jewels. "Sir, I'm bound by my vow to Molave."

"You are. Explain your behavior. Why would you break protocol and come to me unrequested?"

Sitting on the edge of the chair with my ankles crossed beneath me, I forged ahead. "Sir, on my way to Molave Palace, I came across a situation in Brynad, inside the Boutch province." I sat tall. "I wanted you" —I gazed at Roman— "both of you to hear the news from me."

"What did you do?" Roman's question came forth with all the irritation and determination of the man before him.

The king's gaze narrowed.

"I spoke to a crowd outside a closed grocer's."

While King Theo remained silent, red seeped upward from his shirt collar, turning his neck and cheeks a shade of crimson. His stare fluttered between Roman and me.

"Your Majesty," I went on, "the citizens said the grocer had been closed for three days."

"It isn't your concern, Princess."

"Yes," I pressed forward, "it is. My vow was to you, to my husband" —I looked briefly to my side— "and to the people of Molave. I've asked Roman for years to allow me to help with the people. They listen when I speak." My sentences were coming increasingly rapid-fire. "It isn't my objective to take my husband's place but to be beside him, to help. I'm only able to reflect his light if I'm seen. The people said the markets are now all owned by the royal family. It wasn't so when I was first taught about the country's economy."

King Theo took a deep breath and leaned back against his chair. "The queen stays content with her duties. You can assist her with the upcoming event."

"Yes, sir. I respect that. I will. I also want to do more." I feigned a smile, reached over to my husband's arm, and kept my eyes veiled. "I want to help you, Roman." I swallowed the lump in my throat brought on by Roman's cold response. Turning back to the king, I added, "Your Majesty, it is within your authority to allow me—"

"Everything is in my authority," he said, interrupting. His attention went to Roman. "Why have you not brought Lucille's requests to me before now?"

This was a performance for my benefit.

As Roman responded, the two men weren't the only ones acting. I was also on the stage, needing to convince my king of my desire while maintaining the façade that I had no knowledge of the truth about the man at my side.

Roman was speaking. "...discuss it in private. My decision is made." He stood and puffed his chest. "My judgments are not to be questioned."

My palms dampened and my chin remained high as Roman's tirade continued. Once he was done, I waited, my gaze on the king. Finally, I replied, "I promised the people, sir. I promised to return tomorrow—"

"Absolutely not," Roman roared.

King Theo lifted his hand in silence. "What did you promise, Lucille?"

"I gave my word that I would speak to you. I also promised to return to Brynad tomorrow to see that the grocer's is reopened."

"You don't have that authority," the king said matter-of-factly.

"I'm speaking to you, sir, the man with the authority. That is half my promise."

King Theodore stood and paced by the window near his desk. The way his forehead furrowed and he pressed his lips together, I had a seed of hope that he was possibly considering my plea.

I wanted to turn to Roman, to make contact, to let him know I wasn't trying to harm his role, but instead, I was determined to keep mine. However, with the king near, I stayed mute. Each step in his trek twisted my nerves tighter than a second before.

Finally, he turned our direction. "I will speak with the Ministry of the Interior," King Theo said.

"Lucille is not going back to Brynad tomorrow on her own. I will not allow it," Roman said.

"Once I speak to Lord Rowlings," King Theo said, "I will make my decision."

Taking a deep breath, I allowed my lips to turn upward.

King Theo took his seat and turned his entire focus on me. "Go to Mr. Davies today, Princess. Your health is our primary concern."

I nodded. "I'm well, Your Grace. I believe allowing the people of Molave to see more of me" —I paused—

"especially if the procedure works, will reinforce that the royal family is strong and growing."

"I'm canceling the procedure," Roman said. Still standing, he'd moved closer to my chair. "The king and I were just discussing it."

I replied to the king, not my husband. "Providing an heir is my duty."

"You're dismissed, Princess," the king said.

Standing, I curtsied.

"Go to the physician. From what I've been told, the procedure should not occur for a few more days."

The idea that the king was so closely tracking my ovulation was too upsetting to ruminate upon. "Yes, sir."

"And Lucille."

"Yes."

"Speak nothing of the closed markets with Queen Anne."

"If that is your wish." I paused. "It would look poorly if I didn't return to Brynad as I promised."

"You will have my official answer after Roman and I speak, and after we've spoken to Lord Rowlings."

"Thank you, sir." I turned to Roman and offered a neck bow. "Your Highness."

"We will speak."

While the threat was there, in a matter of weeks, the internal fear of impending encounters had waned.

Another nod to my husband and I turned toward the door. Once free from the sanctum of the king's private office, I remembered to breathe. Beyond the next offices, I found Lady Buckingham. Her eyes opened wide as I came into view.

"Your Highness." Concern was evident in her expression. "Are you well?"

I smiled. "My titles are still intact."

"The king?" she whispered.

My mistress and I spoke quietly as we walked to the prince's and my apartments. The hallways near the king's office were busier than those toward the residence, yet never were we completely alone.

"Was surprised by my forwardness," I answered.

"The prince?"

"Happy wouldn't be a fitting description." I turned to her. "The king mentioned the diplomat banquet."

"Yes, ma'am. It has been on your schedule."

I shook my head. "I feel unprepared."

"No need to worry. I've been in communication with Lady Kornhall. She's assured me your attire is planned and Friday you will meet with the royal jeweler and decide what to wear."

It was all I could do not to roll my eyes. There was no doubt that a lovely gown and jewels from the royal jeweler would materialize in plenty of time. Once we were within the apartments, I told Lady

Buckingham about the king's order to see Mr. Davies today.

"I will have lunch brought to you and call the royal physician's office for a time. The Princess of Molave should not be made to wait."

I reached out and covered Lady Buckingham's hand. "Thank you, Mary. I know you care."

"What of your promise to return to Brynad?"

"His majesty said he'd speak to the minister of the interior and get back to Lady Larsen." Lady Larsen was my personal secretary. "She'll inform me."

"That is far better than I'd feared."

"I had imagined far worse too," I confessed.

I was alone in my apartment with my lunch, awaiting my appointment with the royal physician, when my phone buzzed. Looking at the screen, I read my husband's name. I opened his text message.

"Wait for me in our apartments. You are forbidden from leaving for any reason."

Forbidden.

The chicken pasta salad churned in my stomach as I contemplated my next move. By the time on the clock, I would need to leave soon for Mr. Davies' exam; unsurprisingly, he made time to see me sooner than I planned.

There was a knock as the door to my parlor opened.

"Your Highness, it is time for me to escort you to Mr. Davies."

I looked back down at my phone and up to my mistress. "The prince has forbidden it."

"The king..."

CHAPTER 9

Roman

An hour had passed since I sent the text message to Lucille. With my uncertainty on the privacy status of our communication, the direct order was all I felt comfortable sending. That's not to say that there weren't copious thoughts going through my head that I wanted to relay; most presumably, the words I was thinking were inappropriate for the princess's ears, especially if our communications were monitored.

For nearly the last two hours, I sat at the king's side as Lord Rowlings and his assistant, the Duke of Hampshire, briefed us on the status of small markets and supply-chain glitches.

I would rather have Lucille to myself in Monovia, but unquestionably, the Molave Palace was where I would learn the relevant and current tensions transpiring within Molave. The king's and my discussion of Borinkia was put on the back burner by more pressing concerns.

Lucille was right to bring the situation to our attention. Although I never acknowledged her behavior as positive to the king, her bravery brought a problem to light that even I hadn't noticed as we traveled through the Boutch province.

While in the king's presence, I overheard an aide informing him that Lucille's appointment with the royal physician was scheduled. I gritted my teeth as I waited to be informed. The message wasn't relayed. That was when I sent the text.

Now, with Lord Martin at my side, I was headed up to our apartments.

"Your appointments are waiting, sir," he reminded me for the third time.

"I will tend to those after the matter of the princess."

We were almost to the top of the grand staircase when he spoke in a hushed tone. "It isn't like you, sir, to put the princess above your duties."

Stopping, I turned to Lord Martin, keeping my voice hushed yet stern. "I've watched and read. Roman would not allow what Lucille did today to go without words."

"Words" —he inhaled— "would not be the end of it."

"I know my role."

"The state banquet."

"What about it?" I asked.

"The princess should not be marred."

The small hairs on the back of my neck bristled. "Do not question me about my responses, not when it has to do with the princess." I lowered my volume. "I don't care what an asshole Roman was. I will not raise my hand to her or any woman."

"Harsh words, sir. That will do."

I stood taller. "It will do." We walked along the corridors until the double doors of the princess's and my apartments were in view. "Go to my offices. Have all appointments rescheduled for a half an hour from now. I'm certain you can say whatever is necessary to smooth the situation. After all, I have been in audience with the king."

He peered down at the watch on his wrist.

"Make it work," I said impatiently. "Reschedule some to tomorrow if necessary."

"Yes, sir," he said with a neck bow.

Tugging on the front of the suit coat, I stood tall, pushing my shoulders back and approaching the entry to our parlor. Once inside, I scanned the empty room. It appeared the same as it had been before our trip to Monovia, sans fresh new flowers on the large round table near the entry and a fire flickering in the large fireplace.

Instead of heading directly toward my suite, I went

to the doors leading to Lucille's and without knocking, turned the knob and pushed the door inward.

The princess and Lady Buckingham turned my way with a gasp and wide eyes. Since the princess's arrival in the king's office, she'd changed her clothes, now wearing a pair of soft pants and a long jumper. Her long dark hair was down and damp and her beauty undefiled by makeup.

"Your Highness," they said in unison as they both stood and curtsied.

My focus stayed on the princess as my command came forth, "Leave us, Lady Buckingham."

Although I'd been rehearsing my rebuke in my head, the raw beauty of the woman before me rendered me speechless. As the doors closed, leaving us alone, I couldn't resist the pull to go to her. With less than a meter separating us, Lucille cast her gaze downward.

"Are you here to admonish me?"

"Yes," I replied, my tone less than harsh.

She lifted her chin and spoke softly. "You promised to help me."

"Helping you is setting you free."

Lucille shook her head. "Helping the citizens is what I need to do."

"Your appointment?"

"I didn't go. My husband forbade it."

A smile lifted my cheeks as I cupped one of hers

with my palm. "Lord Martin warned me that you will be observed at the state banquet, and I should keep my rebuke to words."

Lucille's face inclined to my touch. "I want to help you succeed." Her lashes fluttered as she closed and opened her blue eyes. "But I won't be discarded, Roman. I'm not being replaced."

The divorce.

"I spoke to the king about it," I confessed.

"What did he say?"

"At first, he tried to pretend there wasn't a plan in the works, but then he admitted that Roman was in talks with Alek Volkov."

Lucille lowered her chin.

With a thumb and finger, I lifted her face until her blue orbs were visible. "What reason did you give the royal physician's office?"

"The truth."

"I suppose that will be the next discussion I have with the king. He's aware of my displeasure." I took a step back and scanned Lucille from her hair to her bare toes. "You never wear shoes."

"I do. I recently finished my bath in preparation for tonight's dinner."

"Yeah, fuck," I mumbled. "Dinner with the king and queen will be fine. Friday evening..." I tilted my head. "I could use a crash course in state banquets. Are you available to be my teacher?"

Her smile blossomed. "Only if you'll stop talking about divorce."

I shook my head. "Can't you see? I want you safe. America is safe."

Lucille came closer and reached for my hand, entwining our fingers. "Together is safest, Roman."

Earlier this morning, I left this woman in tears, resolving to save her by sending her away. In the hours that passed, my determination had lessened. Snaking my arm around her waist, I brought her hips to mine. Tilting my head forward with our lips millimeters apart, I spoke. "The only part of you I'll ever bruise are your luscious lips."

Her blue orbs sparkled. "If kissing is my punishment, I fear I'll continue to misbehave."

"Then I'll need to find more grueling punishments," I said as my lips took hers. She tasted sweet like toothpaste and any thoughts of admonishing this stunning, strong woman in my arms faded away.

When we pulled apart, my smile returned, and I ran my thumb over her pinkened lips. Looking up to her gaze, I spoke low. "It's far too dangerous for you to travel back to Brynad."

"I was just there. It wasn't dangerous."

"You announced that you'd return." I sighed. "Your

speech from earlier today is already making the social media circuits. You gave the time and date of your return. You provided an invitation to those who wish us harm."

The princess shook her head. "I didn't mean..." She sighed. "Roman, I must keep my word. If I don't...if the people lose faith in me..."

"I shouldn't say but I was privy to the king's discussion with Lord Rowlings. The stores will receive stock overnight and open for a few hours each day until more supplies can be secured."

"That's good."

I ran my thumb over her cheek. "It's because of you, Princess. Your bravery at confronting the king is truly inspiring."

"Roman, I can't stay in Molave Palace and ignore the king's and the physician's orders."

"Let me speak to Mr. Davies."

"And then what?"

"I don't know," I answered honestly. "I'm winging this from minute to minute. I do know that as Roman Godfrey, I have power. I've spent the last six weeks using that power as I'm told. I don't think it's too much for me to use that power to protect you."

"From what? Pregnancy? It's what all Molave wants."

"What do you want?" I asked.

Lucille took a step back. "Roman, please don't."

"Don't what?"

"Don't pretend or mislead yourself into believing my feelings matter. They don't. When I see Rothy and Alice, I admit to wanting children. When I see the people, such as those in Brynad, I want to help them. If the procedure fails, I've failed, and I won't be able to help the citizens of Molave."

"I will ask the king for a month. He has said I should work to repair our relationship. I'll ask for one month."

Lucille nodded.

The vibration of my phone in my suitcoat pocket alerted me to the fact our time together was running out. I took Lucille's hand and lifted her knuckles to my lips. "You were strong and fierce today. You were also reckless and put yourself in danger." I looked down at her sparkling wedding rings and back up to her. "As your husband, I'm responsible for advising you. My advice is to continue being strong and fierce, and to never again put yourself in danger. If the king permits your return to Brynad tomorrow, I will accompany you as will a convoy of guards." One more kiss to her knuckles. "I don't want to leave you, but as my phone keeps vibrating, I'm reminded that I'm late for a horrible afternoon filled with meetings."

"Tonight, if you call for me, I'll do my best to prepare you for the state banquet."

I nodded. "The only way this will work is if we are one another's top advisor."

"No more talk of divorce," she said.

"As long as you heed my advice."

"Is that a threat, my prince?"

Stepping closer, I whispered in her ear, purposely warming her sensitive skin. "I love you, Lucille. I wish to God I didn't, but I do. Don't be reckless with what I love."

When our gazes met, a single tear slid down her cheek.

"Princess?"

"I'm afraid to hope that we will succeed."

"Hope is all we have."

Brushing her lips with mine, I turned and made my way out of Lucille's suite. To my relief, the connecting parlor was empty. It wasn't until I neared the back stairs that would lead closer to my offices that I saw Lady Buckingham.

"Your Highness," she said with a curtsy.

"The princess is waiting for you."

"The physician's office called."

"Not today. She isn't up for it."

Lady Buckingham's expression soured as she nodded. It would be up to Lucille to do her part in convincing her mistress of her distress. I couldn't accept that Lady Buckingham turned the other cheek to Roman's abusive behavior, but I could appreciate that she was Lucille's guard, her protection. With Lady Buckingham at her side, within the walls of the castle or palace, the princess was well cared for.

"Your Highness," the secretaries addressed as I entered the front office.

Lord Martin appeared from one of the conference rooms. "Your Highness, Mr. Davies is here to see you."

"Good."

"The king has been told you stopped the princess from seeing the physician."

"I'll speak with the physician now and undoubtedly, the king later."

Despite the concern in Lord Martin's expression, he nodded a bow before opening the door to my inner office.

CHAPTER 10

Lucille

Moonlight flowed through the windows like glowing blue ink, lightening my bedchamber. Although the hour was late, I wasn't tired. Since Roman's rebuke—the thought of which left my lips tingling—we'd not had a moment alone. His dreadful afternoon of meetings lasted later than usual. By the time I was ready for dinner with the king and queen, Roman had just enough time to change into a new suit and escort me to the dining room.

There were too many people about for us to speak, and it was clear that we were going for the impression that the prince was still upset about my behavior. It was a fine line to walk since around Queen Anne we also weren't to mention anything about my findings or speech in Brynad.

While King Theo, Roman, and I sat mulling over what had transpired, Queen Anne talked throughout most of the meal, excited about Friday night's royal banquet. It had been since last spring that Molave Palace had such an event. I knew from experience that the preparation literally took months. When King Theo said the queen was content in her duties, one of them was preparing for pomp and circumstance—a responsibility she didn't take lightly. No doubt the grand hall was already set with tables and chairs, and the next few days would be spent making sure each goblet was set precisely in place as well as every piece of silverware. And then there were the flowers and napkins. The to-do list was exhausting, and Queen Anne oversaw every aspect.

I longed to speak to Roman about the upcoming festivities. He'd asked for my help. That said, I was certain Lord Martin and Lady Caroline had done their part to prepare him for such occasions.

As I paced about my bedchamber in my dressing gown, I waited for a sign from Roman. I'd asked him to call for me, but he hadn't. Now with the clock nearing eleven, I was beginning to wonder if he would come to me, if he were truly upset with me—as he appeared at dinner—or if simply, his busy afternoon had worn him out.

My lips curled upward at the sound of doors opening and gently closing in my outer parlor. Anticipation built within me, much like the sensation of waiting for the curtain to rise on a Broadway show. The knob on my door turned moments before the door pushed inward.

"Princess," Lady Buckingham said. "You should be asleep."

The crushing disappointment at seeing my mistress was almost more than my roller coaster of an emotional day could handle. Blinking away the moisture in my eyes, I nodded. "I am about to be."

She went to the bed and pulled back the covers. "Let me help you."

"Why are you here?" I asked.

"After this afternoon...I was concerned. The prince's reaction wasn't unexpected..." She took a deep breath. "I was hoping to find you sleeping soundly."

When Lady Buckingham had come to me after Roman left, I pretended to be upset at his rebuke while at the same time, trying to stay strong. It was what I would have done before. And before, I would have settled into my bed and perhaps read, hoping to not receive a summons.

Now, I wanted the summons, and it hadn't come.

Taking off the robe, I slid under the covers in my long pale-pink nightgown. Instead of being a thirty-three-year-old woman, I was a child being tucked into bed.

"Goodnight, Mary," I said.

"Goodnight, Princess."

My thoughts filled with Queen Anne's musings about the upcoming banquet. I was almost asleep when the clicks of doors opening and closing pulled me from the grip of slumber. Sitting up against the headboard, I pulled the blankets over my body and watched the door to my bedchamber open.

In the darkness, I only saw Roman's silhouette, framed by the light from the fireplace beyond.

My breathing evened as I took him in—his broad shoulders and trim torso told me that the padded shirt was gone. If I were to guess, I'd say he wasn't wearing a shirt at all. The door closed behind him, and his silhouette faded into the darkened corners of the room.

The anticipation from earlier returned as the prince came silently toward me, walking through streams of blue hue.

By the time he was at my side, I inhaled the scent of his bodywash. Warmth radiated from him to me as he sat at my side, causing the mattress to dip. In silence broken only by the sound of our breathing, Roman lifted his palm to my cheek.

"You're awake."

It wasn't a question. The answer was obvious.

"You didn't call for me," I said, inclining my face to his touch.

"That's because I'm still upset with you."

"Are you?"

"No."

My smile grew as my eyesight adjusted, and I took in his bare wide shoulders and toned chest. "I love you, too."

Roman's touch disappeared.

I reached for his hands and held them between mine. "You have no commitment to me. I know that, and yet being with you feels as it should when I'm with my husband."

"I met with Mr. Davies."

"And?"

"You will see him, but the procedure will wait another month. For now, he only wants to confirm your temperature and ovulation charts." Roman shook his head. "I still think this is wrong."

Warmth filled my cheeks. "It's an odd conversation considering our short history. The real Roman...the one before you...he would never have discussed this with me." I smiled. "I think it's better to hear it from you than Mr. Davies...or King Theo."

Roman chuckled. "The king offered to have our marriage blessed by the Church of Molave."

"He what?"

"Yes, he said it was a usual practice after times of difficulty in a marriage."

"Difficulty, such as replacing my husband with another man."

"I think that would qualify."

Roman lowered his forehead to mine. The fresh scent of toothpaste infiltrated my senses as I pondered the king's offer.

"Would that make our marriage so?" I shook my head. "You didn't agree to this job to end up with a wife."

"I didn't."

"It wouldn't be fair to you or Roman."

"He's still the greatest unknown. Where is the real prince?"

"I don't know," I replied, knowing that no matter how unfair it was to the real Roman, the Roman I wanted was holding my hand, breathing the same air, and making me desire only him. It wasn't only this Roman's beauty, his now-verified Hollywood appearance and defined muscles. My desire stemmed from what we were doing now—talking.

I remembered something from earlier. "I researched you."

"You did what?"

"You told me your last name. I searched for you."

"Lucille, the Firm will see that and know you know."

Shit.

My pulse increased and my skin grew clammy. "I-I wasn't thinking."

"Obviously," he said, dropping my hand and standing. "We need to come up with a story."

Quickly, I scooted out of the bed, meeting Roman where he stood. "I'm sorry I acted impulsively. I wanted to know more about you. You've spent the last two months learning about me and Molave." I lowered my chin. "I am sorry."

Roman reached for my shoulders. "No apologies, Princess. Hopefully, I'm paranoid. Maybe they aren't monitoring your searches."

When he released me, I walked one way and then the other as I tried to come up with a way to pacify the Firm. My eyes opened wide. "I saw an advertisement for the next movie in that comic series, the one where you're a warlord. I noticed the resemblance to my husband, and that's why I searched the actor's name."

"That could work. Although, I'd never noticed the similarity before I was approached."

Looking up, I studied his handsome face. The man within my reach wasn't a prince but a fictional warlord. "You'll need to return. You have a career."

Inhaling, he ran his hand over his hair and exhaled. "I've been killed."

My head tilted.

"The Firm approached Andrew after I'd shot my last scene in the franchise."

"The ad I saw on the internet had you listed as having a major role."

He shrugged. "My demise was a recent change and as far as I know, a secret."

"You don't think the Firm was involved in the script change, to make you available?" Now I was sounding as paranoid as Roman.

"I hadn't thought of that." He walked to the window and back. "I don't know how far-reaching their power goes. At the time, I had another explanation for the studio's decision."

"What was it?"

Roman turned to me with a sad smile. "Irrelevant. No longer important." He hooked my finger with his. "Just like you, Princess, I made a vow. The past is the past. I'd like to say that my survival is no longer at the discretion of a director or producer, but I think we both know that wouldn't be a true statement." Dropping my finger, he wrapped his arms around my waist and pulled me against him. "Our future is in the hands of King Theo. Survival is a day at a time. Will you help me prepare for the state banquet?"

"Yes," I answered, looking up into his dark stare. "I'll help however I can."

Suddenly, Roman moved, reaching for one of my hands while keeping his other arm around me. In seconds, we were dancing, waltzing around the room to music that only Roman could hear. I was too taken with his actions to even think of telling him there wouldn't be dancing at the banquet.

His direction was impeccable and his touch sensual. Our bodies moved in sync, as he guided us in and out of moonbeams.

Roman's tenor lowered as the bedchamber filled with his baritone hum.

In his arms, dancing to the tune of his melody, the world around us slipped away.

Never had I had a dancing partner as talented or as confident. I was enthralled as the walls of my bedchamber disappeared and Roman's dark gaze drank me in.

It didn't register that dancing and singing were most likely talents that he'd honed through his profession. I was too entranced. The man commanding my attention had my body attuned with his in a way I had never dreamed possible, as well as my heart in his hands.

If only the world could witness the new romance between a married couple who had drifted apart. It would be a second-chance sensation or maybe only a replication.

A reflection was only as strong as the looking glass.

As we continued to waltz, I refused to believe the mirror could break.

Little did I realize how soon our reflection would be threatened.

CHAPTER 11

Lucille

Cool autumn air swirled, tingling my cheeks, as Lady Buckingham and I made our way outside Molave Palace to the waiting cars. Much to my surprise, I'd received the king's approval to make a return trip to Brynad. The news came earlier this morning, giving my mistress and I a short time to ready for travel. The small town was less than a half an hour from Molave City's limits. I was approved to arrive before noon, the time the market was scheduled to open.

With the colder temperatures, my attire was less important than the impact of my presence. This was the first time in all my years as princess that I'd been given such a responsibility. I knew in the grand scheme of the Molavian people, one small speech was insignificant.

To me, it was monumental.

My presence was requested by the minister of the interior and chief minister soon after word arrived of my granted request. Lord Rowlings and Mrs. Drake met with me for a short time, going over what I was to say. I respectfully listened to their advice before asking, "What does the crown not want me to say?"

The two ministers looked at one another and back to me.

"I'll gladly relay the speech you provided," I replied. "However, if I'm asked questions, I want to be able to answer."

It took a little prodding, but the perimeters were set. In a nutshell, I would deliver a speech thanking the citizens for their patience and explain that the unusually early onset of cold temperatures had resulted in ice in the channels, causing shipping delays. In the few hours I had to prepare, I'd gone over and over the outline. As we approached the cars, a mixture of emotions bubbled within me, excitement being the one that undoubtedly was in the greatest supply.

Breaths appeared as small clouds as the guards opened car doors.

"Wait."

I spun at the sound of the familiar voice. "Roman?"

"Princess."

Remembering protocol, I curtsied. "Your Highness."

We hadn't seen one another since our dance last night in my bedchamber. The memories of our waltz warmed me from the inside. Before I could say another word, my husband reached for my elbow and pulled me away from Lady Buckingham and the guards.

He spoke low. "I don't approve of this journey."

My elation at having permission to do something for the citizens of Molave evaporated such as the popping of a balloon. Inhaling, I looked up to my husband's dark stare, wondering for a moment if this was a performance for those around us.

"The king." I looked toward the cars. "I'll have royal guards."

As I spoke, I looked up at his handsome face. The rigidness of his chiseled jaw and intensity of his dark stare were real, not an act.

Roman lowered his voice. "I don't approve, but I'm not forbidding it."

"Thank you," I said with a sigh, "Your Highness."

"I'm going with you."

"Can you? Does King Theo approve? What of your schedule?"

Roman lifted his chin toward the cars. "We should go." He spoke louder. "There has been a change in plans. Lady Buckingham, you may stay here. I'll accompany the princess to Brynad."

Lady Buckingham curtsied and muttered the appropriate response, yet the entire time, her gaze was on me. I went forward and reached for her hand. "Enjoy an hour to yourself."

She forced a smile. "I know you'll do well. I wanted to see it."

I turned to Roman. "Perhaps my mistress could ride with me and you..."

Roman shook his head. "Lady Buckingham is welcome in one of the other cars. I want to hear what you plan to say."

Nodding, I smiled at my mistress. "It's your decision. Stay or you may ride with the royal guards."

Once Roman and I were in the back seat of the royal vehicle, I spoke low. "Does the king know you're with me?"

"He will."

I shook my head. "Roman..."

His hand covered mine on the seat between us. "As soon as I was told that you had met with Lord Rowlings and Mrs. Drake, I hurried to find you." His dark orbs focused straight ahead, but his tone and timbre made my heart beat faster. "I want you to succeed, Lucille."

"They don't?"

"The jury is out." He feigned a smile as the car began moving. "Now, tell me what you plan to say."

For the next half an hour, I spoke and Roman critiqued. It wasn't negative but instructional, refining some points and giving me additional background on others. By the time we arrived in Brynad, Roman's aid increased my confidence.

The crowd was larger than it had been yesterday. No doubt, word had gotten out that the market would soon be open. As the caravan approached, Roman again covered my hand with his. "I believe it's best if you speak first." He tilted his chin. "Only after the guards are confident that you're safe."

"Who would want to hurt me?"

"Don't think about that now. Think about what you plan to say." His cheeks rose as his lips curled. "Show them your heart, Princess."

I swallowed the lump in my throat. "Thank you."

My ears rang with cheers and the sound of my name as a guard opened the car door and I stepped out. To my surprise, Roman stayed within the car. I hadn't realized when he'd said first, he meant alone. Taking a deep breath, I stood tall. This was my plan all along. I never dreamt he'd join me.

With a long wool coat covering my blouse and slacks, my hands covered by leather gloves, and high-heeled boots on my feet, I made my way to the front door of the market.

"Thank you, Princess," a woman standing nearby said.

I lifted my hands. "First, let me thank you. Each

one of you who was here yesterday. I'm sorry I wasn't aware of your plight. Thank you for informing me."

"Did you speak to King Theodore?" a man asked.

"I did as I promised. The good news is that this grocer's as well as those in Deca and Gekfjord will today and onward, each day be open for three hours." The crowd murmured. "The crown appreciates your patience as the cold weather has caused delays in shipping."

"For how many days or weeks will the stores be open for only three hours?"

"What of those who are working during those hours?"

The questions came from all sides.

Utilizing what Lord Rowlings and Mrs. Drake had shared, I did my best to answer what I could. It was one question that prompted a new speaker.

"Where is the prince? Does he approve of what you're doing?"

The back door to the vehicle opened and Roman stepped out. The crowd that had gotten louder grew eerily silent as they parted, allowing the prince to step to my side. He looked over the crowd.

"I believe someone asked if I approve." Roman's gaze came my way as a smile formed. "Your Princess brought her concerns for you to the king and to me as soon as she arrived at Molave Palace." He grinned. "I approve."

The crowd began chanting my name.

Roman lifted his hand. "The crown is working with Parliament to form commissions in each province to have direct communication with a royal director. The crown shouldn't be informed of your difficulties or successes because they are accidentally observed. The commissions will form means of communication with the foreign affairs ministry who will in turn report to me."

The people listened as Roman spoke. Many of the older citizens nodded their approval. As elated as I'd been to speak, standing beside Roman, watching and hearing his sincerity, filled me with a new sense of pride. Not only for what we stood for as prince and princess but also for what we could accomplish.

When he finished, Roman looked at me. "Princess, I believe it's time to let these good people shop."

I lifted my hand to wave.

The door behind us jingled as we started to step away.

With a royal guard at my side, the heel of my boot caught on something. Stumbling forward, I reached out, trying to balance myself.

The door to the store opened.

Still unsteady, I gasped as people lunged toward

me. Lost in a sea of people, I searched for my husband and the guards. With guards leading him away, Roman faded into the crowd. The people came from all directions, lurching as I tried to back away.

My arms covered my face, as I fell to my knee, and the crowd surrounded me.

A stampede.

Pushing and shoving.

Unable to fight, I closed my eyes and concentrated on righting myself.

A vise-like grip of my arm came, lifting me to my feet and hurling me against a solid wall.

It wasn't a wall.

I peered upward as Roman's brow furrowed, and he cradled my face against his chest.

The royal guards gathered and surrounded us as we moved in a pod toward our cars.

It wasn't until Roman ushered me into the back seat that I finally caught my breath and found my bearings. The door behind us was closed, muting the sound of the crowd, as Roman's gloved hands framed my cheeks. His intense stare swirled with shades of brown and black as he looked directly into my gaze.

"Lucille, are you hurt?"

"I-I..." I stammered as I looked over myself and my husband. "I think I'm well."

His jaw clenched as he ran a gloved finger over my

cheek. When he pulled it back, the leather was red. "You're bleeding."

I reached up, touching my cheek.

"Get the princess a bandage," he called to the guards in the front seat as the car began to move.

Carefully framing my cheeks, Roman held my face as his lips landed on my forehead. Warmth from his rapid breaths covered my skin.

His soft words were for my ears alone. "I turned around, and you were gone. I was so fucking scared."

"It all happened so fast." I pulled away from his hold as the car began to move, focusing on Roman's dark orbs. "It was an accident. They didn't mean to hurt me."

Roman shook his head as he reached for the packet our security offered. A strong scent of alcohol came with a simultaneous sting causing me to wince as he dabbed my cheek.

"I'm sorry," he whispered.

The tears prickling my eyes weren't from the pain. They were from the tenderness in Roman's touch, the concern in his gaze, and the sincerity in his words. "We'll have the physician check you over."

"I'm okay."

Carefully, Roman peeled back the adhesive from the bandage and placed it on my cheek. "This will do until you can get to the infirmary."

I reached for Roman's hand. "Thank you."

Squaring his shoulders, he said, "I never should have allowed this." He tilted his head. "I also agree. The people didn't mean to hurt you. It was a rush on the market." His jaw clenched. "It should have been predicted." Sitting back, he pulled his cellphone from his pocket.

My thoughts were a blur as he spoke.

The reception. My speech. Roman's public approval…it was all perfect until…

Once he was done speaking, I turned to my husband. "Who did you call?"

"Mrs. Drake. If this happened in Brynad, there's the possibility for rushes at all the opening grocers. They could even be worse in larger villages. I instructed her to send ministry guards to all the markets and manage the crowds. No one should be injured going to the market."

Despite my still trembling hands, I reached out to Roman's arm and spoke low so as to not be overheard by the guards in the front seat. "You saved me, and you're concerned about the citizens."

"Princess," he said in a whisper, "saving you is my main objective."

"But that call…it was to help the citizens." I spoke softly, a lump of emotion forming within me. "*He* would have been angry. Helping the people wouldn't have been on his mind."

"You were magnificent today," he said with his smile returning. "They love you."

"I should make an official statement."

Roman nodded. "Once we're back, we'll speak with Lord Rowlings and Mrs. Drake. I agree, you should be proactive. Speak about the positive."

As Roman's phone vibrated, I sat back and laid my head against his shoulder. His wool overcoat abraded my cheek as I closed my eyes, and the weight of what happened settled over me.

The rush wasn't about me.

And still, for a moment or longer, I was lost and frightened.

I'd said Roman—the old one—wouldn't have thought about the citizens.

Would he have thought to turn back and save me?

In my heart, I feared the answer was no. He wouldn't have tried to save me because he never would have allowed me to speak in the first place.

Roman's hand came to my leg. "We've been summoned to King Theodore's offices."

CHAPTER 12

Roman

As the door opened and Lucille and I were announced, the king's inner office came into view. With Mrs. Drake sitting opposite the desk from King Theodore, both sets of eyes were upon us as Lucille curtsied and I bowed. After speaking our proper greetings to the king, my focus went to Mrs. Drake. "Have the ministry guards been deployed?"

"Yes."

"Their only mission is to keep the peace," I said.

Before Mrs. Drake could reply, the king stood. Walking around his desk with his focus on Lucille's bandaged cheek, he asked, "Are you harmed, Princess?"

Her hand went to her cheek. "No, sir. More frightened than anything."

The king shook his head. "It was a mistake to authorize your outing."

"It wasn't the people's fault," Lucille began, giving

the king the same speech she'd given me in the car. "...are worried and concerned about food."

Mrs. Drake looked up from her phone. "Your Majesty, there appears to be an unexpected development."

"What now?"

"The video of the prince helping the princess to the car has gone viral. There are already nearly a million views worldwide. The comments are overwhelmingly positive." She turned to Lucille. "The people are concerned about you."

The princess looked up at me and back to the chief minister. "I should make a formal statement. Something to tell the people I'm well and that I understand the incident was unintentional."

Mrs. Drake nodded. "This could work." She turned toward the king. "With everything that's happened recently, this is the most positive press the crown has seen in too long." She looked down and back up. "Prince Roman, the people seem to admire your quick thinking to save your wife."

"It wasn't thinking," I admitted. "It was panic."

"The guards were there," Lucille said, "but it was Roman who got me out of the crowd."

King Theodore reached for Lucille's hands and smiled down at her. "You made Molave proud today. Now, go directly to Mr. Davies. He will make sure your injuries are properly treated."

Lucille curtsied. "Yes, Your Majesty. My mistress is waiting. We'll go together."

"Our office will release a joint statement with yours, Princess," Mrs. Drake said.

"Thank you."

King Theodore spoke, "The queen is expecting your help in the grand dining hall this afternoon. If you're up to it."

"I am, sir."

"Don't mention anything about what happened. Queen Anne is delicate. She has a lot to think about before the state banquet."

"As you wish."

As they spoke, I questioned what I should have questioned sooner. Everyone spoke of the king's health, yet the queen lived in a bubble of his making. Not only that, but her own son had been replaced at least twice before her eyes, and she seemed oblivious.

Lucille nodded toward me before turning and disappearing behind a closing door.

"What the hell happened?" Theodore's voice echoed off the walls. "I didn't approve your accompanying the princess."

"I'm glad I was there," I replied.

"It was fortunate," Mrs. Drake said. "The unexpected response could help the crown. As you know, the prince's popularity was dwindling. *Your* popularity," she rephrased. "Perhaps it would be beneficial for the two of you to make more appearances throughout the provinces and ride this wave of goodwill."

King Theodore sat back against his chair and templed his fingers beneath his chin. His dark stare came to me. "What is your opinion, Roman?"

My opinion was that Lucille had always been popular with the citizens. Not utilizing her talents and glowing personality to their fullest extent was an obvious error of the three people in this office. I didn't verbalize that. Instead, I replied, "My vow is to Molave. If such visits would help, I'm willing."

"What of the princess?"

"If it is your and the ministry's wish, Lucille will abide."

The king inhaled and exhaled. "This could benefit more than the crown. It could help repair what was destroyed before you arrived."

"Our marriage?"

I wanted to ask what that would mean about the Princess of Borinkia. However, with Mrs. Drake present, I wasn't sure of what she knew.

"You want that?" Mrs. Drake asked. She sat tall, her words edged with indignation. "You truly are a man of many talents: learning about Molave, courting the princess, and wowing the Molavian people."

"If anything I've done is unsatisfactory," I said, "I expect to be told."

"No, Your Highness," Mrs. Drake said as she stood, "we're pleased."

If that were the case, she should alert her expression.

I looked from her to the king and back. "Thank you." It was the closest to a review of my work I would get. "In our perfect world, I would assume that Roman would be able to retake his duties soon."

"In the perfect world," the chief minister replied.

"Our world isn't perfect," the king said. "I was informed you have appointments waiting in your office. I wouldn't be surprised if you're questioned about today's incident. Damn social media. There was a time…"

When he didn't finish his thought, I prodded. "And if questioned, I will say…"

"Exactly what was said here," the chief minister said. "The incident was unintentional. You and the princess are safe. Stores are restocking and reopening. All is right with the world."

"Perfect world," I said.

"Not quite, sir," she said with a quirk of her smile. "Improving."

Leaving Mrs. Drake and King Theodore alone, I entered the king's outer offices where Lord Martin was waiting. With his lips pinched together in a straight line, he bowed his head at my approach. For the first part of our journey through the palace corridors, we remained silent. My mind was back in Brynad.

Finally, I spoke, "Why didn't the guards get to her faster?"

"I wasn't there, sir."

My nostrils flared as I recalled Lucille's trembling body as I whisked her to the safety of our car. She believed that together we were safe.

Could this have happened on purpose?
What if she'd been alone?

"Have one of my secretaries contact Lady Buckingham," I said.

"Yes, sir. May I ask what this is about?"

"The chief minister and king think it would be helpful to the crown's PR for the princess and me to visit the provinces affected by the recent supply shortages. Find out which towns and devise a schedule. It will need to be coordinated with both of our offices."

"The king agreed?"

"He did."

Lord Martin lowered his voice. "Your Highness, this is very good news. I was afraid that—" He took a deep breath. "Publicity such as today's isn't usually welcome. The king doesn't appreciate a negative reflection on the crown."

"Such as the Eurasia tour last summer?"

Lord Martin nodded.

I stopped before entering the corridor to my offices. "What became of Lord Avery?"

"Your Highness?"

"I've been asked about him," I lied. "Apparently, he held a position similar to yours."

"Lord Avery retired, sir. I apologize for not mentioning him earlier. You should have been informed on how to respond."

I clapped my hand on Lord Martin's shoulder. "No concerns. I've always enjoyed improv. The audience is more engaged."

"If you fail, sir..."

Swallowing, I felt my Adam's apple bob. "You will be encouraged to retire?"

Lord Martin nodded.

"Then I say I won't fail."

"I'm concerned about the princess."

My neck straightened. "What is your concern?"

"You're attracted to her," he said. "Go slow on your relationship. We can't risk her questioning you—a change in you."

"Slow." I smiled. "Good advice." I tilted my head toward the offices. "Any advice for in there?"

"No, Your Highness. If Mrs. Drake and the king are pleased, keep doing what you're doing."

"Gather a list of villages and provinces, and have a tentative schedule arranged."

"Yes, sir."

CHAPTER 13

Lucille

"Your Highness," Lady Buckingham said as I met her in the outer office. The stress and concern showed in her furrowed brow, pursed lips, and hazel stare.

"I'm fine, Mary."

With a sigh, my mistress closed her eyes. By the time they opened, a stray tear glided down her cheek. "I'll get an ice pack."

"We're on our way to the infirmary. The king and the prince want to be sure I'm all right." Reaching for her hands, I spoke softly, leading her from the king's offices. "This—today—was good. I'm not hurt, not badly." The pain from my cheek was outweighed by the elation from my last conversation. My heart felt as though it was ready to leap from my chest. "The king and Mrs. Drake thanked me for my service to Molave." Leaning closer, I looked into her orbs. "I'm doing something."

"At what cost, Princess? Your safety? Your health?"

"A few scratches. It wasn't intentional. The people wanted to get into the store."

I'd had abrasions before. This time it was for the greater good.

Lady Buckingham slowed her steps as she led me to the side of the grand gallery on our way to the infirmary. "I was in the car with the guards."

"Yes."

"They spoke in a code of some sort, but I had the feeling they expected the crowd to become unruly when the doors to the grocer's opened. I even urged them to go to you. They said there were already two guards at your side. If additional palace guards appeared, their gesture could be misconstrued."

My eyebrows knitted together as I contemplated what she was telling me. "They anticipated the rush?"

Mary Buckingham shook her head. "I can't say that for certain. It was a feeling."

Straightening my neck, I forced a smile. "I'll speak with the prince." I added quickly, "As well as the king, the foreign minister, and Mrs. Drake."

"It wouldn't be good if the guards believed I was telling tales."

"Nonsense. I won't use your name." Except with Roman. I would tell him.

"The guards seemed irritated that Prince Roman was present, from the start."

"I'm glad he was there."

Mary sighed. "Me too, Your Highness. For once, I was."

"Has he seemed different?" I asked, fishing for my mistress's knowledge.

"At times. At times you've been different as well. It isn't my place to say."

"Come," I said, reaching for her arm. "Mr. Davies is waiting."

Different members of the royal staff curtsied and thanked me for my service as we made our way through the corridors.

"Word has spread quickly," I said.

"Social media," Lady Buckingham replied. "It was all the king's secretaries were discussing while you and the prince were in his office."

Entering the infirmary, Lady Buckingham announced my presence to the front clinician. "Princess Lucille is here to see Mr. Davies."

The clinician stood and curtsied. "Your Highness, let me take you back to an examination room."

It wasn't long before Mr. Davies knocked and entered. His focus immediately went to the bandage on my cheek. "Are there other injuries, Your Highness?"

I shook my head as my fingertips went to my cheek. "I don't believe so. Only my cheek. It's tender, but that's all."

"Let me take a look."

As Mr. Davies tended to my cheek, he asked questions about the incident. Once he seemed convinced that I was mostly unharmed, he brought up the usual reason I saw him. "I met with the prince."

My chin dropped. "He doesn't want me to continue with the idea of IUI."

I flinched as the physician cleaned my wound.

Apologizing, he continued his work while speaking. He met my gaze. "Princess, what are your thoughts on the IUI?"

Sighing, I spoke a fear I'd kept close to my heart. "I'm afraid that even it won't work."

"All of the tests say you're fertile."

After opening an app, I handed Mr. Davies my phone. "I've done as you said, keeping track of my temperature upon waking."

The physician nodded. His eyes opened wide as he studied the chart.

"This is today's temperature?" he asked, pointing to the number.

"Yes."

"Princess, I believe you're ovulating."

Simply hearing the words had my pulse racing. He was still speaking, but I wasn't listening. This was my way to remain. If I were to become pregnant, I couldn't be sent away.

"You haven't, correct?"

I shook my head. "I'm sorry, Mr. Davies. What was your question?"

"Sexual relations?"

Never had lying been easy for me. I was honest to a fault. That honesty was what often caused issues between the old Roman and me. Nevertheless, with my new Roman's role—and possibly life—on the line, I shook my head. "No."

"I would like to do an exam."

"Why?"

Mr. Davies lowered his voice. "Princess, if there is any chance you answered that question erroneously..." As I began to speak, he lifted his hand. "Please allow me to continue."

I nodded.

"It would be best to report that the procedure was completed."

My jaw was set as I stared at the physician. In essence he was telling me that it would be better for me if I became pregnant from the procedure than an impostor. Of course, he couldn't tell me he knew that my husband wasn't Roman, not a Godfrey, not an heir. Then again, the last man wasn't either.

"I believe I would know if I'd had relations," I said indignantly.

"Yes, Princess."

I wanted to ask a hundred questions; however, all of them would lead Mr. Davies to the knowledge that I knew Roman wasn't really Roman. "Roman said to wait a month."

The physician's nostrils flared. "As your physician, I will respect your wishes, Princess. I'm not asking your husband or the king. I'm looking at you. If after five years you would miraculously conceive an heir during a time when you and your husband weren't engaged in sexual activities, there would be questions."

"Maybe I conceived last month."

"If you hadn't had an exam and a negative test, that story could be believable."

"Who would need to be convinced?" I asked. "The crown would be ecstatic with the news." When he didn't respond, I asked, "Do you have the sample?"

"Yes. The sperm is frozen."

"Frozen," I repeated, realizing that it made the most sense. Roman's sperm. Regardless of where he was, this had been planned. "How long can sperm be frozen?"

"Years, up to ten."

This was Roman's sperm, the man I married.

Mr. Davies's words broke through the fog of my decision. "...the nurse will prep you. The sperm will be ready in about fifteen minutes."

Wringing my hands, I thought about the outcome. If I became pregnant without the procedure, those privy to the knowledge would know that the new Roman and I had been intimate. If that happened, the child wouldn't be an heir. Maintaining my role and helping the citizens of Molave rested on my ability to conceive.

Specifically, to conceive an heir, not an impostor's child.

With the elation of the trip to Brynad forgotten, I squared my shoulders. "Yes."

"Princess?"

"Thank you, Mr. Davies, for allowing me to make this decision. If I'm ready, if my body is ready, then yes, I'll have the procedure. However, I'd like you to keep this information between us."

"Princess, the protocol..."

"If we have good news to share, you can tell everyone who needs to know the truth. However, if it fails, I'd like the one more month my husband fought for."

Mr. Davies nodded. "As you wish. The nurse will be in soon and help you prepare."

My stomach twisted as the door closed, leaving me alone with my thoughts and fears. I knew sperm lived after sex. Roman and I hadn't used protection, not last night, or the night before, or...

Even with the procedure, I could already be with child.

Laying my palm over my lower stomach, I imagined the possibility.

"I hope you're already there," I whispered. "I'll protect you. This is for you."

The clicking of the doorknob pulled me from my thoughts as the door opened and I met the gaze of a familiar woman wearing purple scrubs.

"Princess Lucille, I'm Lizzy." She smiled. "I'm here to help you prepare."

"Lizzy," I said, "I hope you're good at keeping secrets. I don't want to disappoint the crown."

"Very good, Your Highness."

CHAPTER 14

Lucille

The last two days were a whirlwind of preparation for the diplomats' state banquet. While my office had coordinated with the chief minister's office on a public statement regarding the incident in Brynad, my current duties were no longer as an ambassador for the crown, but instead, that of being Queen Anne's shadow.

Watching.

Learning.

Helping where I could.

Much of the work had already been done.

It took a team approximately four weeks to unpack Archibald III's royal service—plates and over 1500 pieces of cutlery. Each person would have six glasses: water, champagne toast, red and white wines, dessert wine, and port. Each place setting was placed exactly 45 centimeters from the next and every chair was positioned an equal distance from the table. During the banquet, each serving station would be manned by a page, footman, underbutler, and wine butler.

All of the napkins were embroidered with the Godfrey crest and precisely folded by one person for continuity. The meal would consist of four courses that remained a secret until the night of the banquet.

The painstaking precision Queen Anne put into the banquet was admirable.

This was where the queen shone.

Pomp and circumstance was a responsibility she took to heart and one that one day, she wanted me to take over. I admired her dedication, but honestly, planning dinners seemed unimportant compared to what could be accomplished outside of the palace with the people.

Roman's and my offices were coordinating a schedule for us to travel about Molave.

I looked out over the large dining hall, imagining the seats occupied.

The queen was speaking with Lord Frederick, the master of the household. He held most of the responsibility for the banquet; however, nothing was executed without the queen's approval. The menu had been planned for nearly six months, yet recent food shortages and shipping affected Molave Palace, too.

Queen Anne was upset about the last-minute changes.

Walking to where the two were talking, I waited until they were done.

After Lord Frederick walked toward one of the serving stations, Queen Anne turned to me and sighed. "I don't understand how the chef wasn't prepared."

Did she even know about the current problems?

Instead of asking, I smiled. "No one knew the original menu. The change can be our little secret. While we're eating duck, only you and I will know it should have been lamb."

She covered my hand with hers. "Lucille, you are always positive." Small lines formed around her eyes and lips as she smiled. "Thank you for loving my son."

My ears buzzed with her compliment. During the extent of our marriage, she'd never before mentioned love.

"I'm but the moon to his sun."

Queen Anne shook her head. "It isn't always easy. I know that. However, I think Theo was right in calling Roman to Molave City after the Eurasia tour. Roman seems..." She paused. "Calmer."

"He has been less quick to anger of late," I replied honestly.

"He cares for you. I see it. I don't know why I didn't see it before, but now I do." She reached up to my cheek with the small bandage. "My husband thinks I don't know what happens in this country, but I do. I saw the video of Roman saving you from the crowd of people." Tears came to her eyes. "It will be our secret, but I want you to know, of all Roman's accomplishments, watching him react as he did, well, I'm proud."

"You could tell him," I suggested.

"Oh no. If I did, Theo would learn my secret."

"That you are proud of your son?"

"No, dear. That I'm more aware than he thinks." She looked over the dining hall. "One day this will be your responsibility, Lucille. You've told me that you want to do more for Molave." She nodded. "I'd like to think that when you do, because I believe in you, that you won't forget the importance and symbolism of overseeing a state banquet. You probably think it's boring."

"No, Your Majesty."

"Oh, it can be monotonous, but when this room is filled, every detail is worth it. Our honored guests tonight are men and women who work tirelessly for Molave. They deserve to be treated to the extravaganza of this ceremonial affair."

I remembered my awe at attending my first state banquet. There had been banquets given in Roman's and my honor during our recent tour, a gesture toward us. This was part of royal life and the queen had rightfully reminded me of its significance.

"I promise I will maintain this tradition. You're

right. It's important for the state guests to experience the grandeur of the crown."

"Theo was right about you from the beginning." She looked down at her watch. "We need to finish here because it takes much longer for me to be dressed and ready than it will you. Have you chosen your jewels for tonight?"

Tiaras were required at these banquets. "Yes, Lady Buckingham has advised the royal jeweler."

"Diplomats will be present from over forty Molavian embassies. I'm sure you've studied the guest list."

"Yes, ma'am."

"Wonderful." She stared down the long table and spotted the master of household. "I must speak to Lord Frederick about one last detail."

"Would you like me to join you?"

"No, dear. Rest. Our smiles will be weary by the time Theo finishes his meal."

With a neck bow, I smiled. At dinners such as tonight's, the meal was officially over when King Theodore was done eating. No one would leave before. That could mean the night could go on for much longer than our regular dining.

Wearing my dressing gown, my thoughts were on what Queen Anne had said about Roman as Lady Buckingham styled my long hair in an updo, creating the perfect style for the tiara I'd chosen. It was beautiful and originally created for Queen Louise, King Theodore's mother. It's my personal favorite, not only for its appearance but because it is lighter than other family tiaras and more comfortable. The diamond-and-pearl earrings complemented the diamond-and-pearl necklace.

Lady Buckingham looked down at her phone and back up, meeting my gaze in the mirror. "You and the prince have been summoned to the king's office before the dinner."

"Why?"

"I don't know, Your Highness. It is unusual."

"Does the prince know?" I asked.

Lady Buckingham nodded. "Lord Martin is the one who informed me."

I let out a long breath. In all my years, I'd never been summoned to his office before such a large event. Of course, my thoughts went to Roman, this Roman.

"You look beautiful," Lady Buckingham said as she took a step back. "Now, your dress."

I leaned closer to the mirror inspecting my cheek. "You've done a wonderful job covering what is left of the laceration."

"I would say that no one would know, but with the video, you may even be asked about it."

As my mistress zipped the back of my long cream-colored dress, the door to my parlor opened.

"Your Highness," we said in unison with a curtsy.

Roman looked especially handsome in his white tie and tails. Beneath his coat he wore the golden sash and upon his jacket were his ribbons and medals from his time in the royal army. His dark eyes scanned me from my tiara to my toes, hidden beneath the length of the dress.

"We're wanted in Papa's office."

I nodded. "I'm almost ready."

Instead of leaving my bedchamber, as his predecessor would have done, Roman walked to the large windows and waited while Lady Buckingham finished helping me. Once she was done, she bowed her head and smiled. "I will leave you two."

"Thank you," I said. It wasn't until the door closed that I turned to Roman. "What is this summons about?"

He turned to me. "I was hoping you'd know."

"No, never have we been summoned before a banquet. There's too much happening with guests arriving."

"Lord Martin was unsure as well." He came close and reached for my hand. "You're beautiful, Lucille. If

I don't get the chance to tell you that again, know that you are—inside and out."

"Roman, you're scaring me."

"I'm a bit worried. What if my time is done?"

"No," I said, shaking my head. "Not before a banquet. Unless…" My pulse thumped in my ears as I held tight to my husband's hands.

Clouds swirled in Roman's dark eyes as he shrugged. "Unless Roman is back."

CHAPTER 15

Roman

The sheer look of terror in Lucille's blue orbs made me want to take her from the palace and run. I wasn't sure where we would be able to go, but ever since Lord Martin informed me of the summons, the two of us getting away from this madness was all I could think about.

Cupping Lucille's cheek, I feigned a smile. "You'll be okay. You're strong, my princess."

Leaning toward my touch, her eyelashes fluttered before she sighed. "No, it can't be that he's back. King Theo wouldn't want me present."

"Unless he knows you know."

"I haven't said a word." Her hand covered her stomach. "Mr. Davies."

"What about Mr. Davies?"

Lucille spun, the skirt of her dress pitching as she walked to the fireplace.

"You told me he checked your cheek and said you were well."

She nodded.

Going closer, I laid my hand on her shoulder. "What haven't you told me?"

When she turned and peered up at me, the color had drained from her cheeks, making her ghostly pale.

"Roman, we need to go. At the banquet, we must talk and laugh. And King Theo..."

"Tell me." My tone was gruffer than I intended.

She inhaled. "The royal physician may think I know the truth about you."

"Why?"

"He didn't believe me that we'd not had sexual relations."

"He called you, the princess, a liar?"

"No," she explained. "He said according to my temperature charts, he believed I was ovulating."

"Three days ago?" I asked, my mind working frantically to come up with our last time to have sex. It would be easier to remember a night we didn't. "You could be pregnant."

She nodded. "He suggested that I go through with the procedure."

"I said no."

"I know, Roman." Desperation infiltrated her words. "Mr. Davies said that if I became pregnant without the procedure while not engaging in sexual relations...don't you see?" She didn't let me reply.

"He was saying if I become pregnant with a child and that child isn't an heir... I couldn't let on that I understood what he was doing, but he was right. If I'm pregnant with your child, the king will never allow it."

"Are you telling me you did it? You had the procedure?" Again, my volume was raised.

"Yes, Roman. I did it. If I end up with a child, the king can believe it happened with IUI."

"But where did they get the sperm?"

"I believe it was Roman's. Mr. Davies said it was frozen. He said sperm can be frozen for up to ten years. I checked when I got back here, and the internet said the same thing."

That made it official.

I started to run my hand over my hair and stopped, seeing the sleeves of the black jacket. "Shit, Lucille. When did you plan on telling me?"

"Not now, but if it's my last chance..." Her blue eyes glistened with unshed tears.

My tone softened. "Obviously, Mr. Davies knows I'm not Roman. He examined me upon my arrival. I made it clear to him upon our arrival back to Molave Palace that I didn't want you to undergo the IUI. Maybe he put the clues together that we're intimate. That doesn't mean he knows you know I'm an impostor."

She nodded. "You're right. We need to go to the king."

Reaching for Lucille's hand, I lifted it and left a kiss on her knuckles. "Whatever comes, I won't leave your side."

"Then the banquet will be the talk of Molave. Princess Lucille and two Prince Romans."

"How are you feeling?"

Lucille shook her head. "No different."

This was crazy.

I took a role to play a part, not to have a child.

Shaking my head, I said, "This is certainly a fucked-up situation."

"You should have left after our first meeting. You could be safe in the States."

"I was ready to, and then we spoke." I wanted to tell her that she would be safe with a divorce, but I couldn't bring myself to say the words, not after the way they upset her days ago. Instead, I offered her my arm. "Come, my princess. We will meet whatever awaits us together."

On our way through the palace corridors, Lucille told me what Queen Anne had said, that I seemed calmer. Perhaps I should be more boisterous, but that personality was exhausting. Over the nearly three months, I'd tried to tone Roman down in small increments. Apparently, the queen had noticed.

I'd also convinced Lady Caroline that we could slowly decrease the padding in the shirt. While I still wore one, it wasn't as padded as when I'd arrived. If the real Roman was back, he'd need to alter his appearance to match mine.

"She also saw the video of us in Brynad."

"She did?"

Lucille nodded. "I believe she's more aware of things than King Theo gives her credit."

We stopped talking as we approached the king's offices.

The royal guards bowed as the princess and I passed through the first doors and through the front offices. The king's assistant greeted us and led us toward Theodore's private office. Although I'd been in the same room earlier in the day, this felt different.

I looked down at Lucille. "We'll be fine."

Shaking her head only slightly, she pressed her lips together.

"Your Majesties, the prince and princess are here."

Majesties?

"Mum," I said, surprised to see the queen standing near the king.

They were both dressed in their formal white-tie attire. It was the first time I'd seen the queen wearing a crown. They weren't alone. Francis and Isabella were also present.

Lucille released my arm and curtsied.

After bowing, I went to the queen. "You look lovely, Mum."

"Thank you, Roman."

Isabella came forward and gave Lucille a hug.

"I didn't realize you'd be here," Lucille said.

"Papa wanted us here for banquet," Isabella replied.

"Yes, Anne, we have a banquet," King Theodore said.

"Right, right," the queen said, lifting a small box from the top of Theodore's desk. "Lucille, please come closer."

What the hell was happening?

Lucille's blue eyes quickly met mine before she did as the queen bid.

"I know this is unusual timing," the queen began as she held the box, "however, Lucille, you are a blessing and an asset to the Molave crown. This should have been presented to you years ago." She looked over at me and back to Lucille. "I spoke to Theo, and we wanted you to have it before tonight's banquet."

"Ma'am?"

Lucille gasped and her fingers went to her painted lips as the queen opened the box.

"Now, no tears. We have banquet."

I stepped closer and peered over Lucille's shoulder.

"The badge of the royal family order," I said, seeing the blue ribbon with the portrait of King Theodore surrounded with diamonds. I'd learned about the royal family order sometime during my training.

"I'm honored, Your Grace," Lucille said.

"Here, son," the queen said, handing me the ribbon. "Help your beautiful wife with her well-deserved badge."

Francis and Isabella's expressions were neither positive nor negative as they observed the informal ceremony.

If this was one of those moments when I should be rude or abrupt, I failed miserably. I was too in shock that our summons was a positive thing and more so, by the grace and strength of the woman I called my princess.

Opening the pin on the back of the ribbon, I scanned Lucille's dress and had flashbacks of being an awkward teenager trying to pin a corsage on a girl for prom. Lucille's laughter filtered through the air like a melody.

Feeling the warmth in my cheeks, I stepped forward and after placing my fingers behind the fabric of her neckline, I slid the pin in and out. "You deserve this," I whispered as I clasped the pin.

"Did you know?"

"He was the reason you hadn't received it," King

Theodore said. His booming voice caused the three of us to turn his direction. "However, after Brynad, Roman and I spoke. Afterward, I told Anne I thought he would no longer object."

"You objected?" Lucille asked.

It wasn't me.

I would never.

"You heard him, no longer." I kissed her forehead.

"Did you know?"

This time I answered, "I didn't know you'd receive it tonight, but I'm glad you did."

Lucille looked down at the badge, covered it with her hand, and turned to the king and queen. "I will wear it with honor." She curtsied. "Thank you. I will remain in Molave's service."

Queen Anne whispered something to Lucille who smiled in return.

King Theodore stood. "It is nearing time for our procession." He reached for Lucille's hands. "Thank you."

"Sir?"

"We Godfreys aren't always the easiest men."

I offered Lucille my arm. "My princess, shall we?"

"Roman and Francis," King Theodore said. "If the queen and princesses would give us a minute."

Lucille, Isabella, and Queen Anne nodded, going out of the inner office and closing the door.

"Is there a problem, sir?" I asked.

"Our ambassador to Norway informed me of a development with Borinkia. Tomorrow first thing in the morning, Mrs. Drake and I will have a formal meeting with him. I want you both present."

My gaze went to Francis. "How does this affect him?"

Francis nodded. "I'm sure I wouldn't have been invited if my presence was irrelevant."

"Yes, sir," I said to the king. "I'll be there."

"As will I."

"Then we should go to banquet," the king said, gesturing for Francis to step ahead of us. Once he was through the doorway, the king looked my direction and spoke low. "Your mother mentioned that you seem calmer."

I didn't respond.

"Don't stay too calm," he warned.

"I shall throw a plate at the banquet."

King Theodore laughed. "Perhaps another time."

"The royal family order," I said, "wouldn't be given to the princess if I were expected to divorce her."

"Let's not get ahead of ourselves."

The questions grew as we joined our wives.

CHAPTER 16

Lucille

The Molavian national anthem played as Roman and I followed a few paces behind King Theodore and Queen Anne. The Duke and Duchess of Wilmington were behind us. The guests stood, rising from their seats, bowing and curtsying as we passed. For a sliver in time, I completely forgot the man at my side was an impostor. As he nodded his greeting and recounted names of different guests, he was my husband, the man I'd vowed to love.

My earlier talk with the queen brought new meaning to what we were doing.

Yes, I still wanted to help the citizens of Molave in more fundamental ways.

Looking down, I suppressed a snicker as I recalled Roman describing us as playing dress-up or make-believe. Seeing him in his formal attire with his medals and ribbons, I realized we were playing dress-up, especially him. And still, the eyes of the guests in the room were fixed on the six of us.

Even what we were doing now was helping the people.

This was part of our job.

One of the butlers pulled out my chair as another one pulled out Queen Anne's and Princess Isabella's. Once Roman, Francis, and King Theodore were seated, the room of people also took their seats. The king gave the first speech, followed by Mrs. Drake. Lord Landon, Molave's ambassador to the United Nations, had the next address, and Molave's representative to the Security Council was the final speaker.

Champagne was poured into fine crystal stemmed glasses all around the room.

Everyone waited until King Theodore reached for his glass. Once he did, everyone in the room stood. It was Lord Landon who gave the opening toast. Glasses were raised in salute before taking a sip. Protocol had guests sitting between each royal. Even though Roman was a few seats away, I felt his gaze as I lifted the champagne to my lips.

Pretending to drink, I tipped the glass before setting it back down.

My lack of consumption wasn't due to fear of his wrath but the reality that whether by him or the procedure, I could possibly be pregnant. There had been too much happening to give that scenario more thought.

I was seated between Mr. Drake and Molave's ambassador to the United States. Customarily, we spoke with the person on our right during the first course and the left during the second, alternating back and forth.

Geoffrey Drake was a good conversationalist, but it was Dame Sydney Robinson whose company I thoroughly enjoyed. This wasn't our first meeting, and I found myself more than a little homesick for the States after listening to her stories. I'd spent a fair amount of time in Washington DC, where she currently resided, due to my father's work in Congress.

Following our final course, when King Theodore laid his napkin on the bottom of his plate, the room grew silent.

After his farewell message to the guests, we all stood, ready to follow him out. On our procession out of the hall, I stayed beside Dame Robinson, caught up in our discussion.

It wasn't until we were all gathered in one of the elaborate parlors that I thought about Roman. I'd been so involved in my duties and conversations I'd forgotten to worry about him. Now, gazing at him from across the room, I realized there was no need to be concerned.

He was standing and speaking with Lord Landon.

Seeing him in his role as prince and future king filled me with the same feelings I'd had before we were married. It was a concoction of pride, admiration, and attraction. I hadn't realized those feelings had gone away, but they had. And now they were back.

Turning, Roman's dark stare met mine as he smiled and went back to his conversation.

"It appears the rumors are untrue," Dame Robinson said.

"I'm sorry, what rumors?"

"There is talk in the States that you're unhappy in your marriage."

I lifted my eyebrows. "Surely, the people in the States have better things to discuss."

"Oh, you're always a topic of discussion, Princess. I was hoping that gossip wasn't true. You know, people love to believe in fairy tales."

"Well, real life is a bit more complicated."

"You just blushed when Prince Roman smiled at you." She leaned closer. "I wish I had a picture. The Americans would eat it up."

"The king has spoken about a tour in the States."

"I was told."

My eyes opened wide. "You were?"

"Yes, there are many logistical and security issues

to plan. I told Lord Landon I believed it would be successful as long as..." Her lips came together.

"As long as..." I prompted.

"The prince. I suggested he stay in Molave and that you would do a solo tour."

I shook my head. "That would never be allowed."

"That's all right. If what I'm witnessing is real, something has changed since the Eurasia tour, and the crowds will love you. I'm working with the planning committee. Is there anywhere you want to visit?"

Sighing, I said, "Home. New York City."

"I'm sure that can be arranged."

Roman appeared at my side.

"Your Royal Highness," Dame Robinson said with a neck bow.

"Dame Robinson." Roman's accent was spot-on as he spoke with the ambassador from the United States. Their discussion continued the one we'd started, talking about possible destinations throughout the States. It wasn't until a Los Angeles stop was brought up that I noticed Roman's stance stiffen.

Of course.

Los Angeles would find us in familiar country for Roman—for Oliver.

"The destinations will need to be cleared with our offices," I said with a smile. "I'm sure it will be lovely."

"In the past," Dame Robinson said, "the affairs

have been much like this." She looked around the palatial room. "To show the States and the world that you are a modern couple willing to take the monarchy forward, I suggest less stuffy venues."

"Is this stuffy?" Roman joked.

"A bit," Dame Robinson admitted.

"What are you proposing?" I asked.

She shook her head. "I truly have only been thinking. However, I would suggest a basketball game while in New York. Perhaps a hockey game in Chicago or a museum."

"That's not stuffy," I said with a smile. "I love the Met in New York City."

"Let my office do some investigation. I'm imagining something as when the Prince and Princess of Wales are seen at Wimbledon. It's about letting people see you enjoy everyday activities." Her eyes opened wide. "I know, a movie premiere in Hollywood."

"Is that something everyday people enjoy?" Roman asked.

"I suppose my ideas need a little work."

I nodded. "I'm getting excited already, Dame Robinson. Thank you. Our offices will be happy to consult with you and Lord Landon. Oh, and the king's office, of course."

"Of course."

Roman nudged me in time to see King Theodore

leaving the room with the queen. "I believe," he said, "that's our cue."

Dame Robinson bowed her head and looked back up with a smile. "Whatever is happening, I approve and so will the American people."

Roman's dark gaze came to me questioningly before turning back to the ambassador. "It's been a pleasure."

"It has, Your Royal Highnesses."

"Shall we, my princess?" he asked, offering me his arm.

The sea of people parted as heads bowed and people wished us good night. As when we entered, Francis and Isabella were behind us. It wasn't until we bid goodnight to the king and queen, that Isabella reached for my hand.

"We will leave midday tomorrow. I'd like to see you in the morning."

"I'd like that," I replied honestly.

It wasn't until Roman and I were on our way up the grand staircase that my husband reached for my hand and questioned me.

"Are you sure you can trust Isabella?"

I peered around, making sure our conversation was not being overheard. "I believe so." That said, I wouldn't share the truth about Roman.

"What did Dame Robinson mean—whatever is happening?" Roman asked.

Feeling the warmth of his hand surrounding mine, I replied, "I think we should take the king's advice."

"Which advice would that be?"

"The cardinal's blessing from the Church of Molave. According to Dame Robinson, there are rumors of our discontent. Based upon her observations tonight, she believes those rumors are false." Warmth filled my cheeks as I turned my head, meeting his gaze. "She said the people would love to see us happy."

"At a basketball game?" he asked in jest.

"Or a movie premiere."

"That can't happen."

CHAPTER 17

Roman

"Good night, Princess," I said as we entered our apartments.

"Your Highness," Lucille replied with a curtsy as long lashes veiled her sparkling blue eyes.

For longer than I intended, I watched Lucille and Lady Buckingham walk across the parlor toward the princess's private suite. I studied everything about the princess. The long cream dress accentuated Lucille's slender waist, the full skirt undoubtedly had layers of material beneath, and the scooped neckline showed a hint of her pert breasts. With her hair fixed in an updo, the diamond-and-pearl necklace and earrings showcased her long neck and collarbone. The diamond tiara was still in place as she paused at the open doors and peered over her shoulder with a smile and a nod.

I imagined helping her from the long dress and revealing her silky skin and soft curves I knew to be hidden beneath. In all my years, I couldn't recall being as affected by one woman. I'd costarred with some of whom the world considered to be the most beautiful and talented actresses. I'd held them in my arms and made love separated by a protective guard. Some of the women I genuinely cared about. Others were simply co-workers, but never had one of them entered my heart.

Maybe Rita, but even so, never had my mind wandered into subjects such as marriage and children. Truly, those thoughts had eluded me.

Lucille Sutton Godfrey was more than the caricature I'd watched on my telly, and with each passing moment in her presence I desired to be the man at her side. Above all, I longed to keep her safe from the ugly workings of the crown.

Tonight was a show.

This was the fairy tale of royalty.

The jewels.

The gowns.

The royal pins of service.

While I'd spent the last three months learning the role, actually experiencing the grandeur of the formality was different than I'd expected. I knew that I was an impostor, yet with each conversation and meeting, that line between acting and reality was growing less distinct.

"Your Highness," Lord Martin prompted.

With a nod, I walked a step ahead of him into my private suite.

A crystal decanter filled with bourbon was now set atop the highboy.

"A drink, sir?" Lord Martin asked, walking toward the cabinet. "In celebration."

"Celebration. What are we celebrating?"

"The chief minister and king are pleased with your performance tonight. The king is encouraged for the upcoming summit."

"And you were informed of this by whom?"

"Sir Connery," my assistant said as he poured two fingers of the amber liquid.

"The king's personal attendant."

"Yes," Lord Martin replied, handing me the crystal tumbler.

As I swirled the contents, I contemplated the subtext behind Lord Martin's compliment. My true identity was known by more and more people at each turn. At least, my false identity. Brushing that thought away, I took a sip and asked, "What is the latest on the PR tour around Molave with Princess Lucille?"

"It's late, sir. Tomorrow, I'll bring you the tentative schedule." Lord Martin came near and took my glass, placing it on the highboy. Next, he began removing my suit coat, complete with the medals and pins. Next, he unfastened the cuff links.

"Is there something wrong with the schedule?" I asked.

"No, sir. The concern is with a few of the proposed locations." Lord Martin continued to speak as he undressed me. "Villages in the southwest have experienced delays with shipping. Their markets have not reopened. Lord Taylor is concerned about safety, especially this close to the summit."

"Tomorrow I'm supposed to meet with the king, duke, and the Molavian ambassador to Norway."

"If I may," Lord Martin said.

I was now down to wearing only my slacks and a white t-shirt, the one covering the padded shirt. I retrieved my drink. "If you know something that will help, you always may."

My attendant took a step back, laid my clothing on a chair, and clasped his hands behind his back. "Prince Volkov is formally objecting to the summit."

"Borinkia isn't part of the Fifteen Eurasia Summit."

"Over the last several years, their government has petitioned to be included. Since that petition hasn't been granted, Prince Volkov is arguing against the meeting of the Fifteen Eurasia Summit in Norway, so close to the Borinkia border."

"Arguing? Is that a threat? Why haven't I been told about this before?"

"The news came only today via the ambassador."

"Why would the Duke of Wilmington be invited to this meeting?"

Lord Martin's gray eyes narrowed. "I suspect it is due to his Norwegian heritage. I'm not sure. I can try to learn."

"Thank you, Lord Martin. Any information will be useful during tomorrow's meeting."

It was nearly an hour later by the time I was finally left alone in my bedchamber. Wearing the satin pajamas with the Godfrey crest, I made my way through the darkened apartment and into the connecting parlor.

Listening for voices, I waited.

After a few moments, I ventured forward, opening the door to Lucille's suite. Her front parlor was dark, a telltale sign that Lady Buckingham was no longer present. Despite the frequency of our nocturnal visits, my pulse sped and my heart thumped as I approached her bedchamber.

Turning the knob and pushing the door inward, a beam of blue moonlight illuminated the bed, and more importantly, the stunning woman asleep within. I hadn't expected her to be sleeping. Now, seeing her, I was drawn closer.

Lucille's long dark hair was down, brushed, and silky in the moonlight.

Her pink lips were parted and her eyes closed.

The banquet had been exhausting, especially for the queen and Lucille. I couldn't bring myself to wake her. Instead, I leaned forward and gently kissed her head. "Good night, my princess."

Lucille's eyes fluttered as she rolled toward me. "Oh, Roman."

"Shh," I prompted. "I shouldn't have wakened you."

She scooted to the side and lifted the blankets. "I was trying to wait for you." Her soft blue stare peered up at me. "Please join me. It's cold."

No longer wearing the formal dressing, Lucille's slender form was covered by a long white nightgown with lace straps and a high lace waist. In the dim illumination, I could see her makeup was gone, revealing her natural beauty.

Slipping into her bed, the warmth of where she'd been sleeping radiated through me as I pulled the blankets back over the two of us. After Lucille's head was settled upon my shoulder and my arm was wrapped around her frame, holding her close, I spoke. "I was thinking."

"About what?" she asked.

"Dame Robinson said the people in the States saw our discontent?"

Lucille nodded. "She said there are rumors that I'm unhappy."

Securing her chin between my thumb and finger, I lifted her face toward me. "Are you?"

"Not any longer." Her eyes closed. "This isn't fair to you. I understand if you don't want our marriage blessed."

"Lucille, I'm a thirty-eight-year-old man who has never proposed." That made me think. "How did I do it? How did I propose?"

Rolling until her arms were on my chest and her beautiful face was above mine, Lucille smiled. "It was very romantic."

I ran my thumb over her cheek, taking in her expression. "I think this is one of the first memories I've asked you about that doesn't make you sad. Your smile is radiant."

Lucille inclined her cheek toward my touch as her smile waned. "I don't know what is real anymore. Was it Roman who proposed? What happened to him? Who was Noah?"

Wanting to see her happy again, I said, "Tell me about the proposal."

"We were in New York City. We'd only been on a few dates. At our first meeting, I didn't know who you were. You introduced yourself as Roman. Never could I have guessed you were a prince. In all honesty, at that time I wouldn't have been able to pinpoint Molave on a map."

It was strange to hear her speak of Roman as if he were me.

"So," I said, "you're saying I swept you off your feet."

"You were intense, but not like later..." She took a deep breath. "When we first met and you'd look at me" —her smile returned— "it was like a movie. My stomach would do flip-flops. I felt special."

"You are special, Lucille."

"I feel it again, with you. I understand that you're only pretending—"

I laid my finger on her soft lips. "Stop. I'm pretending to be Roman Godfrey. I agreed to that. I'm not pretending with you." My palms framed her cheeks as I pulled her lips to mine.

Warm and sweet, our kiss lingered.

When we separated, Lucille's gaze sparkled. "It was late at night. We'd had dinner and seen a show on Broadway, the musical *Chicago*."

My eyes opened wide. "At the Ambassador?"

Lucille nodded.

"Tell me again the year you were married." After she did, I said, "Go on," shocked by the smallness of our worlds.

"After the show, you had a car waiting. It took us to the Empire State Building."

"Cliché."

She scoffed. "I suppose, but at the moment I still didn't know that you were going to propose. We walked right up to the elevators. I was too infatuated to notice the lack of people waiting in line. I later learned the deck had been restricted due to security." Her eyes opened wider. "Oh, things have been so busy. There is something Lady Buckingham said that I meant to tell you."

"Is it about the proposal? Something that will keep that gorgeous smile on your face?"

Lucille shook her head.

"Then let it wait."

Inhaling, she brought the smile back to her lips. Her blue eyes seemed as if she were seeing the memories she was about to describe. "When the elevator opened to the observation deck, there was only a guard and a saxophonist. His music was the perfect backdrop. As we talked about the sights in the city, you dropped to one knee. You said you found me in my country, and you didn't want to return to yours without me."

"I like that that memory makes you happy."

She laid her head on my chest. "Those memories used to make me sad, wondering why things had changed." She lifted her head and turned to me. "I can't make sense of why Roman was replaced, but I can look back and see the good times." Inhaling,

Lucille let her forehead fall to my chest. "I'm afraid of losing you."

Hugging her against me, I held her tight.

"I was there," I finally said.

"What?" Lucille said, sitting up. "Where?"

"Billy Flynn in *Chicago* for three years. Based on the date you said you were married, I was at the Ambassador Theater the night he proposed. You watched me perform."

"That's crazy."

"I agree."

"And then you became the popular warlord."

I shook my head. "I wish you wouldn't have researched me."

"No one has said anything."

"Nor to me," I admitted. Rolling us, we stilled when Lucille was looking up at me with a halo of dark hair around her beautiful face. "You were stunning tonight. I wanted to be the one to help you from your dress."

"That would have been more exciting than Lady Buckingham."

A laugh came from my throat. "I'd prefer you to Lord Martin, also."

CHAPTER 18

Lucille

"I'd planned to let you sleep," Roman said, teasing my long tresses away from my face. "Now, I want you awake."

"I want to be awake."

"It's been a long day."

I palmed his cheeks. "If Your Highness is willing, I'm ready for a longer night."

"No man in his right mind would say no to that."

"Are you in your right mind?" I asked teasingly.

"Obviously, not." His lips met mine. "I'm still willing."

With the weight of his body over mine, I stretched my neck, bringing our lips together as our bodies came to life.

In the last few months, Roman had done more than return my feelings of pride, admiration, and attraction. He'd awakened a feral desire that left me continually longing for his touch.

The fresh scent of soap surrounded us as our skin

warmed, leaving us slick with perspiration and desire. The mint of toothpaste awakened our tastebuds as our tongues danced a tango of giving and taking. My lips would be bruised in the best of ways. Undeterred, I pushed back, giving as much as I was getting.

The way Roman's hands possessively caressed as they roamed over my skin heated my circulation. His intimate presence was like the striking of flint against steel, sparking flames to life. In what had been dry, infertile ground, buds were sprouting, the bursting open of pine cones, only doable by intense heat.

A wildfire of epic proportion.

The flames consumed us, burning away our unfamiliarity and leaving us in ashes of intimacy. We moved in sync as if tuned into one another's desires.

There was no need to think, to consciously tell myself what to do. Those days were gone. Within me, every molecule reacted as endorphins flooded my bloodstream. Nerves and synapses sparked as sensations detonated from my scalp to my toes.

I was alive in a way I'd never been.

A ravenous carnivore desperate to survive.

Feral.

Wild.

Primal.

Untamed.

Being with this man tore down my carefully

constructed walls of isolation. In his presence was where I wanted to be—morning, daytime, and nighttime. Ours was a connection I'd only dared dream could exist.

Piece by piece, our articles of clothing disappeared within the sheets or onto the floor. Their destinations weren't our concern. Instead, it was the unquenchable hunger to be skin on skin. Disrobing one another was not a one-man job as we both tore at buttons and lifted satin material over each other's heads.

My fingertips ran over the indentations of his muscular shoulders and down his toned back and firm buttocks. Such as an unseeing person, I sought to read Roman Godfrey with braille. I wished to touch every centimeter from his salt-and-pepper locks to his strong thighs, lingering on places in between.

His erection swelled under my touch. The velvety skin stretched as I ran my fingers over the slick tip. We moved and rolled to better give and take.

The days of dutiful missionary sex were a distant memory.

Unhindered by protocol or conditioning, I licked the saltiness of his skin and tasted the sultry flavor of his essence. In his embrace I was both predator and prey. The dichotomy was invigorating and freeing.

There was no right or wrong.

We were but two parts of a union that had an undeniable connection.

Instead of fighting what the world had given us, we embraced it, reveled in it, and found joy.

Roman's words of praise and adoration echoed throughout my bedchamber, their power fueling me on and making me believe that fantasy could become real.

In times such as these, I forgot the truth of our lives, lost in a cloud of lust as Roman's lips skirted my exposed skin. His tongue licked, his teeth nipped, and his lips kissed. The stubble of his cheeks would leave red patches that I welcomed. It was as he made his way down my body, spreading my legs, and lapping my essence that I called out.

Lights flashed and shooting stars danced behind my closed eyelids as the pressure within me grew to the point of boiling, and my body stiffened. His hold of my hips was unyielding as he continued his ministrations, adding his long fingers to the pursuit.

I writhed with his touch. His rhythm was my focus as I submitted to pleasure over and over. By the time we became one, my body was wrung out, a ragdoll of overstimulation. Yet as Roman filled and stretched me, my back arched and my heels dug into his lower back, bringing back my energy I'd thought depleted.

In his embrace, I was a dancer in one of his shows.

Choreographed to bring about the greatest ecstasy,

I was in the hands of a master—a star. The more he gave, the more I wanted. Never could I recall my libido being so strong or my desire as insatiable. I was addicted to the pursuit of the next flash of fireworks, the next earthshaking orgasm, and the next empowering roar of Roman's appreciation.

Yes, he was a magnificent lover.

The greatest source of my satisfaction came in his.

Opening my eyes and viewing the way Roman's expression contorted as he neared his release was bliss. The rumble of his roar reverberating through me as he stiffened and filled me with his seed was as close to paradise as I'd ever been.

Lost in the bubble of our making, we dozed and woke again. The night ticked by as we each submitted to our desires. Time and again we came together. The frenzy simmered. Our contact slowed. We took pleasure in the tender pace as our lovemaking continued.

With my arms around his neck resting on Roman's broad shoulders, I waited for my heart to regain its rhythm and my breathing to settle. Lulled almost to a state of satiated unconsciousness, Roman peppered my cheeks with kisses.

"I was almost asleep."

"If I don't leave soon, Lady Buckingham will find us in the tangled sheets."

I tightened my hold. "I don't want you to go."

He brought his nose to mine, his dark eyes staring into mine as the continual tick of the clock threatened to ruin our night of bliss. "I want to ask you something."

I nodded, the seriousness of his tone brought back what I'd wanted to tell him. Before I could speak, he did.

"I'm sorry we aren't in a more romantic place."

"I told you not to apologize," I said. "And I can think of no place I'd rather be."

Roman cleared his throat and lowered his forehead to mine. "Lucille, will you marry me?"

"The blessing?" I asked, my thoughts scattered by the shock of his proposal.

"I will honor that commitment as I honor my commitment to the crown and Molave," Roman said. "I don't want you to think of me as pretending. This—you—us is as real as I've ever been. It's a crazy situation."

"Can I marry another? Isn't that polygamy?"

"Only if Roman is still alive." Roman rolled back to the pillow at my side. "You haven't answered," he said, staring up at the ceiling.

Holding the edge of the blankets to my chest, I stared up at the ornate woodwork in the palace ceiling and contemplated his question—his proposal.

The bed shifted as he moved back the covers.

"I should go."

"No," I said, scooting and sitting up against the headboard.

"No?"

Roman was an Adonis standing completely nude at the side of my bed.

I shook my head. "No, please don't go. Yes, if it is possible, I want to be married to you. I accept. I just don't know."

Still unclothed, Roman knelt on the large mattress and crawled toward me. His broad shoulders shifted with each movement, giving me the sensation of a lion approaching his meal. His lips brushed mine before his gaze locked onto mine. "My princess, the crown has made a farce of your vows. It pains me to be so blunt, but it's true. We can play their game and receive the blessing. But know in my heart, it isn't a mockery what we will be doing. It will be our commitment to one another."

"The divorce?" I asked.

"It was to save you."

"And you'd have been willing to marry Inessa?"

"I don't know. If it guaranteed your safety, then yes."

I reached for his hands. "My prince" —I liked that phrase— "I have fallen in love, in lust, and in awe of you. I wished you into being, and I'm scared you will disappear."

"Then, Lucille Sutton, marry me. No matter what happens, we will keep our commitment to one another."

"What if I wake one day and you are gone?"

He sighed. "I wish I'd read more of Noah's journals. He knew from the beginning that he would either succeed or be replaced. I won't keep the truth from you. If I am afraid that replacing me is in the works, I will tell you, and then together we'll decide our next move."

A smile curled my lips. "The partnership you propose is what I've always wanted." I swallowed. "Yes, I want the blessing."

CHAPTER 19

Roman

I barely made it back to my bedchamber before the morning sounds of waking began to register from the outer parlor. Lady Buckingham would find Lucille asleep dressed in her long nightgown beneath orderly bedclothes. Unless she'd fallen asleep in mere minutes, Lucille would most likely be only pretending to slumber. It had taken the two of us at least fifteen minutes to locate our various items of clothing and remake the bed. The princess also made a trip to her bathroom to remove further evidence of our long night.

When she returned into the bedchamber, her hair was brushed and her smile radiant. She looked down at her shoulders and breasts as a rosy hue filled her cheeks. "Perhaps in the future, you should shave before joining me."

Dressed in my pajamas, I snaked my arm around her waist and pulled her to me. "Tell Lady Buckingham you believe you have a rash. An allergic reaction to the strawberries from last night."

"I'm not as good at lying as you."

"It's not a lie, Princess. It's a fabrication to justify the evidence."

Stretching onto her tiptoes, Lucille softly kissed my cheek. "Good morning, my prince."

I walked her back to her bed and covered her with the blankets. "Good morning, my princess."

"Will I see you at breakfast?"

Shaking my head, I replied, "I doubt it. I have an early audience with King Theodore, the Duke of Wilmington, and the ambassador to Norway."

"Francis?"

"Yes."

"Why?"

"I don't know more," I said. "Be careful with Isabella. Last night, I felt she was watching me."

"You didn't mention that before."

"Because, Princess, you had my thoughts dominated with your presence."

The pink in her cheeks brightened. "I'm sorry, Your Highness, for keeping you from sleep. It sounds as if you have a busy day."

"That is never an apology you need to make. What can you tell me about my relationship with Francis and Isabella?"

Lucille shook her head. "Strained would best describe it. Isabella and I have become friends, but she thinks you're a pompous ass."

"I'd have to agree. I'm working on that."

"Not too fast. People will question."

"That's exactly what King Theodore said last night."

"He did?" she asked.

"What about Francis?"

"To my knowledge, very little interaction. I remember that you walked with him to find me after Rothy's birthday dinner. I was with Isabella in their apartments. I didn't think about it at the time, but it was as if you'd been discussing something."

"It wasn't Roman at the celebration."

"Right?" Lucille said, her eyebrows knitting together. "I don't know. Once you and I were back to our apartments, you were cross."

I shook my head. "Did Noah know his time was about up?"

Lucille placed her finger on my lips. "Do not say his name."

"Please be careful around Isabella," I repeated.

"And you around Francis."

"What did you want to tell me last night?"

Lucille looked toward the clock. "It was about the

guards in Brynad." She squeezed my hand. "It can wait."

A few minutes later, I slipped back into my bedchamber and into my bed.

My mind was a flurry of memories of our long night and concerns over what she hadn't said. There were also more pressing matters within the cyclone of thoughts. There was this morning's meeting. Francis's presence. The odd looks I felt Princess Isabella was giving me last night. The issue of Borinkia objecting to the Fifteen Eurasia Summit. New information that Prince Volkov had petitioned for entry into the summit. As well as the information from the States from Dame Robinson.

Pretending to sleep was ridiculous.

Throwing back the blankets, I stalked to the windows and pulled back the drapes. The sky hadn't yet received the memo that it was morning. At this latitude, the hours of sunlight were waning with each passing day. Thankfully, the temperatures had risen enough to keep the southern provinces free of snow. I would need to check the forecast for the mountains farther north.

Depending upon how this morning's meeting went, I might need to get back to Annabella Castle before the summit. If Noah had information that would help me—help Molave—I needed to learn it.

"Your Highness?" Lord Martin questioned as he entered my bedchamber. "You're awake. Is everything all right?"

"I have a lot on my mind."

"I'm sorry if you didn't sleep well."

Turning back toward the window, I let my smile sneak out. "No time to complain." I sobered my expression and returned my gaze to my assistant. "I'm ready to bathe and dress. The king is expecting me."

"Breakfast, sir?"

"Have it brought in here. And coffee. Black."

"Sir, you drink tea."

I shrugged. "Today, I'll have coffee, the stronger the better."

"Yes, sir. I'll call the butler and then assist you."

Less than an hour later, I was dressed and ready for my day—a day in the life of the Prince of Molave.

"Your Highness," Lady Caroline said with a curtsy, entering my personal parlor.

"Lady Caroline."

"The king would like you present at nine this morning in his office."

I peered down at my watch. At some point my lack of sleep would catch up with me. In the meantime, I was fueled and ready an hour and a half before my curtain call. "I'm going down to my offices." I turned to Lord Martin. "Bring my daily schedule and information about the upcoming PR tour. I'll arrive to the king's office on time."

"There is a matter," Lady Caroline said, "I've been tasked with discussing."

"We can discuss it on our way."

"Your Highness, it is sensitive."

I looked at Lord Martin. "Should you leave?"

"It's up to you," he said.

"Do you know what Lady Caroline is about to say?"

"Yes, sir, I do."

"Fuck, then stay." I turned to her. "On with it."

"It's about the princess."

"Go on."

"She underwent the procedure with Mr. Davies."

As I began to let out a breath at hearing news of what I already knew, I stopped. Raising my volume, I complained, "I forbade it."

Lady Caroline nodded. "It is why you were to be told."

"Who approved this procedure?"

"Sir, it seems the princess did."

"Lucille went against my command." I narrowed my gaze. "Does the king know?"

"Mr. Davies believed that sharing of knowledge would be at your discretion."

I turned to Lord Martin. "Find time in my

schedule for Mr. Davies today. I want to discuss this in person."

"And the princess?" Lord Martin asked. "Will you speak to her about it?"

I already had.

That couldn't be stated.

"Add the physician to my schedule, and get me everything else I've asked for." I looked down again at my watch. "Have a butler bring tea to my office." This morning's coffee was welcomed, but I'd have a larger audience in the offices. "I have a little over an hour before my presence is requested with the king."

As I approached my offices with Lord Martin and Lady Caroline in tow, I was met by an unexpected visitor.

"Roman, we should talk."

I straightened my neck and squared my shoulders. "There's nothing that can't wait for our meeting with Papa."

Francis smiled. "We both know that isn't true."

The key factors when performing improvisation was the ability to play off the other person, to catch each and every context clue, and to respond in a believable period of time. There were no rewrites or second takes.

Keeping my expression stern, I nodded to the

guard at the door to my inner office. As he opened the doors, I said, "Come inside."

CHAPTER 20

Lucille

Roman's warning regarding Isabella echoed in my thoughts as I made my way to the duke and duchess's apartments. I'd been invited to eat breakfast with the duchess. Through all my years of marriage, I'd come to think of Isabella as a friend, perhaps a sister. I didn't like that in the short span of time since my prince had entered my life, I was questioning every relationship I'd thought solid.

Lady Buckingham knocked on the outer door to Isabella and Francis's apartment within Molave Palace. As Isabella's mistress, Lady Johana, opened the door, I caught the gaze of Roman's sister across the room.

"Lucille, I'm so glad we have a chance to catch up."

Nodding to Lady Buckingham and Lady Johana, I went to Isabella. She rose and wrapped me in a hug.

"Sit," Isabella said, gesturing to the table set for two. "Mum never makes it to breakfast the day after banquet. She'll probably be in bed for a few days. And as you may know, Francis and Roman have been commanded to Papa's office."

"The queen works very hard. She deserves rest," I said as I took the seat across from Isabella. "I had no idea you and Francis were coming to banquet."

"I'm surprised Mum didn't mention it. She wanted me here earlier to follow along as she measured the distance between place settings." Lifting her cup of tea, Isabella smiled. "I'm sorry you were dragged into the mundane planning."

"It's important to Queen Anne and one day, it will be my job."

Isabella lowered her voice although since Lady Buckingham left the apartment, the only other person present was her mistress. "Please tell me that the boring old traditions will be gone once Roman is king. Molave needs to move forward, not stay stagnant in time."

Lady Johana poured my tea and brought me a covered plate. When she lifted the silver dome, my usual breakfast of oatmeal, fruit, and toast was served. "Thank you." I turned back to Isabella. "I suppose that will be up to Roman." I looked around. "It's too quiet here without Rothy and Alice."

Isabella smiled. "No sense making them travel to be stowed away in the apartments. Children aren't welcome at banquet. I think I was fourteen when I attended my first."

"Really?"

"I'd heard horror stories from Roman about how dreadfully boring they were."

"He never told me that," I said.

"Of course, it was when he was younger. By the time I was fourteen, Roman was away at University."

I dabbed my spoon into the oatmeal. "He never discusses his youth."

"You said you two barely speak."

Looking up, I met her dark gaze. "It's mostly true."

"Mostly?"

If Roman and I were going to make this work, we both needed to be laying the groundwork.

"I was dreadfully lonely when King Theo called Roman here to the palace after our Eurasia tour." I shrugged. "Whatever the king has done seems to be working." I forced a subdued smile. "Things are improving."

"Things?" Isabella questioned.

"You saw him last night at banquet. He seems" —I used the word Queen Anne had— "calmer."

Isabella shook her head. "Mum has told me as much. I didn't believe it was possible." She leaned over the table. "In Papa's office, with the royal family order, Roman seemed almost happy for you."

Resilient Reign

"I couldn't say. I was so shocked that I barely remember."

"I watched him off and on during banquet," Isabella confessed. "I must agree, he seems happier."

Recalling our long night while eating a bite of toast, I would have to agree.

"Lucille," Isabella said, "if you knew something about Francis, I'd want you to tell me."

The small hairs on the back of my neck rose to attention, such as tiny soldiers ready for battle. "I don't know anything about Francis."

"Mum doesn't know."

Whatever it was, the queen might know more than she'd been given credit.

"Know what?" I asked.

"There are rumors." Isabella took a deep breath and threw her napkin on the table. She turned to her mistress. "Leave us."

As Lady Johana bowed her neck and disappeared beyond the main doors, the small amount of food I'd eaten churned in my stomach. "You're scaring me."

Isabella stood and paced to the fireplace. Opening a small box, she removed some folded pages and came back to me. "I didn't want to believe it. Then I saw this." She handed me the paper.

My hands trembled as I took the pages. Ripped

from a magazine, the pages were folded. Tears came to my eyes as I stared at what still didn't make sense.

"Lucille, you deserve to know."

Inhaling, I unfolded the pages and unfolded again. The words weren't registering as I concentrated on the picture. Three months ago, I would have known without a doubt that the man in the photo was my husband. Too much had changed in three months. While the true identity of the man was unknown, I recognized the woman. I'd looked her up when Roman mentioned divorce.

"Inessa Volkov," I said, allowing the words on the page to come into focus. The words weren't helpful. The article was written in Norwegian. Yet the names stood out.

Roman, Prince of Molave.

Inessa, Princess of Borinkia.

I searched the pages for a date. Looking up at Isabella, I asked, "When was this?"

"It was during your Eurasia tour. This was your stop in Oslo."

In Norway, near Borinkia.

As if the pages were poison, I dropped them, allowing them to flutter to the floor. "He looked happy." It was true.

Isabella stood and reached for my elbow. "You deserve to know."

"And do what?" I questioned louder than I should. "Do you expect me to leave him?"

"No. I have been afraid he'd leave you."

I nodded. "I've heard rumors too."

Her heartfelt words came faster than normal. "Lucille, I watched him last night. I don't know what has changed, but I swear something has—changed for the better. So I didn't want you to be blindsided." She nodded toward the article. "I also hope you two can work through this."

Wrapping my arms around my midsection, I stared down at the photograph on the floor, seeing Roman's and Inessa's faces looking up at me. "Others know about this." I met Isabella's gaze. "The world knows."

"I'm afraid there has been talk. I'd venture to say it was part of the reason your last tour was such a disaster."

My temples pounded as I paced back and forth in Isabella's apartment. My suspicions had been right. Roman had been unfaithful—well, Noah had. I shook my head as I tried to make sense out of it all.

"It's not an excuse," Isabella said, "but there were rumors about Papa when I was young. I didn't hear them until I was older."

"It's not an excuse." I spun to face the duchess. "What would you do if this were Francis?"

"Before or after I cut off his dick?"

My eyes opened wide. "Is that an option?"

"I'm the rightful princess of Molave. I might find a friendlier court. However, in the court of public opinion, you are preferred to Roman. I still don't think you'd get away with murder."

"Murder," I mumbled.

Had Noah been murdered?

Did it have to do with this?

"Lucille," Isabella said, laying her hand on my arm. "No obstacle is insurmountable when two people are willing to work it out. I'm not saying you should stay. I'm also not saying you should go." Her dark eyes pleaded. "What do you want?"

Sighing, I sat back on one of the sofas and let my chin drop to my chest. "I don't know."

Isabella sat beside me. "Yes, you do."

I looked up. "I want my marriage to work."

Exhaling, she sat back. "Oh, I'm glad. I was ready to support you either way, but I'm glad."

"We know we've had trouble." I shrugged. "We're talking more."

"Did he tell you?"

I shook my head.

"Would he be angry if you brought this up?"

I nodded.

The other Roman would be furious.

A thought occurred to me. Standing, I went back to

the table and retrieved the article from the floor. Looking down at the picture, I grinned. Inessa's light hair was pulled back to a tight bun and her complexion was ghostly white. My smile grew until I giggled.

Isabella was back at my side. "Are you sane?"

"Probably not," I replied. "Look at her." I held out the picture.

"She's not as pretty as you," Isabella said.

"She isn't." I shook my head. "I don't mean to sound conceited. It's that Roman used to complain about my beauty as if it were a weapon to use against him. He outshines her. That was what attracted him." I looked up and met Isabella's gaze. "Roman mentioned having our marriage blessed."

"Wait, he used to? And he mentioned what?"

"Having our marriage blessed by the Church of Molave." I nodded again. "He didn't admit to this." I shook the picture. "But am I wrong to believe that the blessing is his way of wanting to start over?"

"No, you're not wrong. That sounds like my brother, get atonement without admitting to the sin."

Thoughts of Dame Robinson came back. "I feel... embarrassed. Dame Robinson mentioned the people in the States think I'm unhappy."

Isabella reached for my hands. "If you want to work on your marriage, you don't owe anyone an apology. Show them, show the whole world how strong you are and how much you love Roman." She grinned. "It will probably piss him off when you receive the praise, but he deserves it."

"It won't all be praise. We both know that."

"No one walks in your shoes, Lucille. Their opinions will change. The world loved Jackie Kennedy."

"The world's a different place now."

"Molave isn't."

"Maybe you're right. It's time Molave moves forward." I squeezed her hand. "Thank you for being honest with me. Have you spoken to Francis about this?"

Isabella nodded. "He's the one who told me. You have to know, I didn't know when we were here for Rothy's celebration."

"But it happened before that."

She nodded her head. "I didn't know."

CHAPTER 21

Roman

Walking a step ahead, I led Francis into my office. My mind was chronicling everything I knew about the man at my heels.

Married my sister, Isabella Godfrey, four years ago.

Duke of Wilmington, a region of Norway.

Fathered two children, my nephew, Rothy, and niece, Alice.

Currently living in a Godfrey castle in Forthwith.

There was one more thing. It was something Lucille had mentioned. Francis and Roman came together to the duke and duchess's apartment after the birthday celebration. She said it seemed as if they'd been talking.

That was very little to go on as I sat behind my desk. "Papa expects us at nine," I said, motioning to the butler to pour my tea.

"Sir?" the butler asked Francis.

"No, thank you," he said, taking the seat opposite me.

I waited until the butler left. Once alone, I narrowed my gaze. "By all means, Francis, make yourself comfortable."

He smirked as he leaned back in the chair. "I'm having trouble following along. Did Mr. Davies change your meds? What's with the way you behaved in Theo's office last night?"

Standing, I went around the desk and crossed my arms over my chest. "What the fuck is your problem?"

My brother-in-law stood, nearly nose to nose. His light coloring was the exact opposite of the Godfreys. "Alek is becoming impatient."

"Not my problem."

Francis reached out, grasping my arm and then immediately pulled away. "I've been trying to reach you for weeks."

I hadn't received word.

Did that mean he and Roman had a secret way to communicate?

"Oh, yes," I improvised, "that conversation after Rothy's celebration."

"You said you had things under control and then you went radio silent."

I scoffed, shook my head, and walked back to my chair. Calmly sitting, I sized up the situation before me. I could either be spot-on or missing the mark by a hundred kilometers. Either way, I had to go with what I could glean. Lifting my teacup, I grinned. "I changed my mind."

Francis exhaled as he paced behind the chair where he'd been seated. "You changed your mind." He repeated the statement, each time louder than the last.

Finally, I lifted my hand, lowered my tenor, and growled, "Shut the fuck up. Do you want the guards on the other side of the door to come busting in here?"

His light blue eyes opened wide. "There he is. Seriously, what is your problem."

"It seems that it's your problem now."

"And when Theodore asks what we know about the objection from Borinkia, are we lying to his face?"

"My memory is foggy," I said with a smirk.

Slapping his palms on the top of my desk, Francis leaned forward. "Let me refresh it for you."

Thank you.

Instead of saying that, I indifferently looked at my watch. "Hurry up."

"That little offshore account that is growing by the day is ours for the picking once we close the deal. Don't tell me that you've changed your mind, and you've decided you want this bullshit life. Let me remind you, you hate it."

"Who knows?" I suggested. "Maybe they're spiking

my tea. I'm not hating it at this minute. I'm enjoying the show."

"Alek wants Borinkia in the Fifteen Eurasia Summit."

"That would make it the Sixteen Eurasia Summit," I said with a smirk.

There was probably a time when Francis knew how to push Roman's buttons. From all I'd studied, having a raving lunatic in the prince's office would have sent Noah or Roman over the edge. Funny thing, I had new buttons. And I had enough experience to push Francis to the brink, storing every word he said.

"What about Inessa?" Francis asked. "She told me you haven't contacted her in months."

Okay, that caught me off guard.

"I'm here in the palace. My every move is being watched and my calls monitored. She should realize that."

"I've told her, but she's getting worried. If she's unhappy and she tells her brother…"

"You're right," I conceded. "I'll figure something out."

"Isabella said something about you and Lucille doing a PR tour."

I nodded. "It's in the works."

"Get Forthwith on the schedule. Spend the night at the castle. Isabella can occupy Lucille, and we'll arrange a getaway for you and Inessa. Just don't fuck it up with photos this time."

This time?

I needed a fucking pause button, time to confer with my producer, director, and castmates. This information was coming too fast and too far out of left field.

"Does Isabella know about Inessa?" I asked.

"I had to tell her," Francis confessed. "I told her about the article with the picture of the two of you, but not that I was in any way involved. She doesn't need to know that."

How, dear brother-in-law, are you involved?

I said, "She was looking at me oddly last night."

"Yeah, she's not happy with you. Love. Fairy tales. Bullshit. The sooner you and Lucille divorce, the quicker things can move on with the Volkovs. Isabella will understand once it's done."

I clenched my jaw. "It's like I'm a prisoner here. Mum is all about the heir."

"You need to stay strong as you have been. Wait until that heir is half-Borinkian. Producing a kid with the baroness's daughter is a slap in Alek's face. You and Inessa will be the beginning of the union of the two countries."

My molars were ready to crack.

What the fuck had Roman gotten himself into? Not

only himself, but also Molave, and most importantly, Lucille.

"Alek's objection," I said, "get me up-to-date before we walk into Papa's office."

Francis shook his head and sat back in the chair. "Don't fuck this up."

"My head's not on the chopping block, brother-in-law."

He leaned forward. "Where do you want me to start?"

I settled against the chair. "Since we don't have time to start at the beginning, start wherever you feel I've lost ground as obviously, you've been more recently informed."

"If you'd check your messages more we wouldn't be in this situation."

Messages?

"I'll look into that. In the meantime…"

✱ ✱ ✱

Francis and I arrived at 8:58 a.m. to Papa's office. While I'd managed to play my role, today's scene in my office was less about my ability to act and more about Francis's willingness to speak. His concerns regarded the deal brokered between Molave and Borinkia, the deal that up until this morning, I was unaware existed.

For only a moment, I recalled the burden of making a producer or director happy. Fuck that. Those were the days. Now I had an entire country and monarchy on my shoulders.

As we walked the hallways, I wondered about Lucille. She was having breakfast with Isabella. I couldn't think about that now—the doors to the king's office were open and waiting for us to enter.

"Prince Roman and the Duke of Wilmington, Your Majesty," a guard announced.

After our customary neck bow and greeting, Francis and I entered the king's inner office. King Theodore sat behind his desk, and no one else was present.

"Mrs. Drake and the ambassador?" I asked.

"They're on their way," the king said. "I wanted a few minutes with the two of you."

After what I'd recently learned, I had no idea where this meeting would go.

"Take a seat."

I looked at my watch. "Do we have a timetable? I have other issues that need my attention."

The king lifted his hand. "Tell me when you last had contact with Prince Volkov?"

"I don't recall," I answered honestly.

"Francis?"

"I believe it was last summer."

"You believe?" the king questioned.

"It was last summer during a trip to Oslo."

"What did you two discuss?" the king asked.

"Nothing of importance."

"Were you aware of his plans to formally object to the Fifteen Eurasia Summit?"

"No, sir. This is the first I'm hearing of it."

"Roman," the king said, "you're unusually quiet."

I shook my head. "I had trouble sleeping last night. A lot on my mind."

"Get your mind on this situation. When Viscount Olsen arrives, I want both of you to be involved. With the Wilmington province bordering Borinkia, the viscount will want your opinion, Francis."

"Our policy has been to not recognize Borinkia. I don't think we should falter," I volunteered despite the earlier conversation with Francis. "If their membership in the Fifteen Eurasia Summit comes up for a vote, we would have to vote no."

"Doing so would be a mistake," Francis said. "Borinkia was recently recognized as a member, no longer an observer, in the United Nations. Our proximity is such that we can't afford a hostile relationship." He nodded my direction. "I think we need to pursue a stronger alliance."

Both sets of eyes were on me.

In the past few days, I'd had very different conversations regarding Princess Lucille. The king wanted me to work on my marriage. Francis seemed to believe my marriage was beyond repair, and it was time to move on with Inessa. Now they were both looking at me.

"The US is more important than Borinkia at this time," I said. "We need to walk a thin line. Our number-one priority is not losing the US support."

Francis's nostrils flared as he sat back. "I disagree. The States are not in range if Prince Alek decides to aim a HIMARS rocket their way. Molave and Wilmington are."

I turned to Francis. "Do you think Volkov would do that?"

"I think we should keep him happy so he won't."

King Theodore inhaled. "This is Molave not Wilmington. Officially, we are staying our course. Unofficially, find out what the prince wants. I want no record of it, but the two of you can deal with Volkov." He smiled my direction. "Thank you, Roman. I believe it's time to call in Mrs. Drake and Viscount Olsen. We need to present a united front."

CHAPTER 22

Lucille

Sitting in my parlor, I read over the names of the cities Roman and I would possibly visit. Some would be a mere car ride away, such as it had been to get to Brynad. Others were farther from the capital city. A smattering were closer to Monovia.

"Are the cities set?" I asked Lady Larsen, my official secretary. It was nice to have her in person, as she stayed in Molave City when I traveled to Monovia.

"These are the tentative destinations, Your Highness. I was told to show you the prospects, and you and the prince would make your thoughts known."

"The prince and *I*?" I asked, surprised to have any say.

"Yes, ma'am."

"Who dictated that I'd have a say?"

"Prince Roman."

A smile curled my lips as I read through the list one more time. When I looked up, Lady Larsen was waiting. "Thank you. Once the prince and I have a chance to discuss this, I'll get back to you."

"I want you to know that security will be increased after what happened in Brynad."

"It was simply a mishap."

Lady Larsen was close to my age with an uncanny ability to keep me organized. Yes, Lady Buckingham dealt with my day-to-day needs, but Lady Larsen ran my official office. It was her staff who coordinated most of my official duties.

Her comment made me think about what Lady Buckingham had said. "Have you heard anything about the guards in Brynad?"

She shook her head. "Why do you ask?"

"In the moment, I was too frightened to think. In hindsight, it seems the rush should have been foreseen."

"No one would purposely put you in harm's way."

"Roman contacted Mrs. Drake and the ministry guards have kept the markets safe."

"That's what's important."

Once alone, no matter what I tried to do, my thoughts continually went back to the picture of Roman and Inessa Volkov. It was wrong to be upset at the man who would appear at any time in our apartments. He wasn't the man in the picture.

I fought with too many questions.

Was Roman's increasingly abusive behavior meant to push me away so he could marry Inessa?

Had he been in love with her?

Had he treated her kinder?

By late afternoon, I realized Isabella and Francis had left for Forthwith, and I hadn't bid them goodbye. Isabella's news had more of an impact on me than I cared to acknowledge.

I'd managed to do little more than read the list of cities over and over, write a few handwritten notes to attendees of the banquet, and wallow in my barrage of worries. My mind was so consumed that I startled when the door from the connecting parlor opened.

"Princess," Roman said, looking around. "Are we alone?"

The hours of dwelling on the photo caught up to me as I stared at the face of the man I couldn't separate from the man before. It was all too complicated.

Dropping my face to my hands, I let the tears flow, the ones I'd held back since my conversation with Isabella. It didn't occur to me that I hadn't greeted the prince in the manner he deserved. My mind was consumed with what he'd done, what Roman—no, Noah—had done.

In seconds, Roman was at my side, crouched down near my feet. "What's wrong? Are you hurt? Ill? Is it... the pregnancy?"

I shook my head.

Roman reached for my hands. "I have so much to tell you."

Sniffling, I blinked away the tears. "He was unfaithful. *You* were." I clarified.

Roman nodded as he tugged me from the chair to standing. "I'm sorry, Princess," he spoke as he wrapped his arms around me. "It wasn't me."

My cheek landed on his chest. The sound of his steady heartbeat kept time as I struggled to breathe.

"Isabella told you?"

I nodded and looked up. "You know?"

"Francis mentioned it, saying Inessa told him I haven't contacted her, and she's concerned."

"You were in regular contact?"

He shook his head and sighed. "I don't know. I can't ask Francis for clarification."

"Isabella showed me a picture of the two of you together. It was from a magazine." I took a step away and opened a drawer in the long library table, the place I'd put the pages after collecting them from the floor in Isabella's apartment. Opening the folds, I handed them to Roman. "Here."

He took the pages without a word and went to the sofa.

"I'm not sure what the article says. I can only make out a few words."

He looked up, his expression sorrowful. "Isabella didn't tell you?"

"I didn't ask. The picture said enough."

Roman lifted his hand, beckoning me to him.

Instead of moving toward him, I crossed my arms over my chest as my temples pounded. "He didn't love me."

Leaving the article on the sofa, Roman returned to where I was standing. "I do, Lucille."

"He hurt me," I said, my tears returning. "And he's still hurting me. This" —I pointed at the article— "was during one of the first stops of the Eurasia tour. I was a laughingstock and he still..."

Roman pulled me to him.

"It's not right," he said, his words reverberating through me as his hand caressed my back. "None of this is fair to you."

The familiar scent of cologne added to my inability to separate the two men from one another. "It's not," I said, looking up at his handsome face. "Maybe you were right. We should leave. Go back to the States and disappear."

"I can't, Lucille. Roman jeopardized Molave with his covert dealings with the Volkovs. If I leave now, King Theodore won't be able to mend it. If you leave, your father will blackball Molave in the US Senate.

We need the contract with the US, and we can't risk upsetting Prince Volkov."

Blinking, I questioned, "You said *we*?"

"What?"

"You said *we* need the contract with the US, and *we* can't risk upsetting Prince Volkov."

"Molave."

"You're doing what the Firm wanted. You're becoming Roman."

"I can't explain it," he said. "I feel a weird connection when there's none." His smile blossomed. "Except with you. That's a real connection. Somehow, I have to break it off with Inessa and not upset her brother in the process."

"What does Borinkia want?"

"To be recognized. According to Francis, Norway and Sweden are waiting to learn our decision. With the Fifteen Eurasia Summit in Norway, there's concern of retaliation by Borinkia if we don't acknowledge the country and allow their presence, if even in a non-voting capacity. The problem is the US could back out of our deal if we acknowledge Borinkia."

I lifted my hand to Roman's cheek. "Do you think he told her he wasn't really Roman?"

"Shit, Princess, I hadn't thought of that. Francis doesn't seem to have a clue...unless he does."

"What do you mean?"

"Francis said I haven't responded to his messages." Roman shook his head. "I haven't gotten messages. He also said I hate this life, and he mentioned an offshore account. Does Roman hate his life or did Noah hate it?"

I lifted my fingertips to my temples. "This is so confusing." I peered over at Roman. "You don't think you should mention any of this to King Theo?"

"I think we need to go back home to Annabella."

"The summit," I reminded him.

"It's a week from Friday. That gives us time to settle into Annabella and hopefully learn more of Noah's doings. I can fly to Oslo and meet the king for the summit." He lifted my hand. "We could make a few stops on our tour."

"Lady Larsen brought me the list of cities." I looked down and back up. "Thank you. Never before have I been consulted. I think my secretary was surprised."

"She can get used to it, Princess. We're a team."

"Tell me when we're free to go back to Annabella. I'll inform Lady Buckingham."

"Tomorrow."

I nodded, ready to go north.

Roman reached for my chin and lifted my gaze to his. "I'm sorry for what has been done to you. As long as I'm around, you won't be hurt, not by me."

Taking a deep breath, I asked, "Are you going to meet with Inessa?"

"I don't see any way around it."

Tipping my forehead to Roman's chest, I closed my eyes, pressing a tear to slide down my cheek. It wasn't fair to tell this man I was jealous. I recalled what he'd said last night. Gazing up through my damp lashes, I asked, "Do you still want to marry me?"

"Yes, my princess."

"She's a princess."

His thumb caressed my cheek. "She's a princess. You're *my* princess."

"Dinner is being brought to our apartments," I said. "The queen is resting, and I don't want to face...anyone."

"I'm facing you, Lucille, and you're a vision."

Wrapping my arms around his torso, I spoke, my words muffled by his suit coat. "I wish I could stay in your arms forever."

"I'm not letting you go."

CHAPTER 23

Roman

After dinner in our apartments, I went on a search, finally locating King Theodore near his offices. His usual suit was replaced with casual slacks and a thick jumper, making his thick midsection more noticeable. A cap covered his white hair.

"Your Majesty," I said, "I was hoping we could speak."

"Why were you and Lucille not at dinner?"

"The banquet has made her tired. She wasn't up for a formal affair."

"The dining room isn't formal. It's family."

"Yes, sir. We plan to leave for Monovia tomorrow."

He shook his head. "She can't leave until the procedure."

I exhaled. "She's had it. Before the banquet."

His eyes opened wide as a smile spread across his face, deepening the wrinkles near his eyes. Patting me on the shoulder, he said, "That is the best news I've heard. Why wasn't I informed?"

"In the grand scheme, I've been a bit preoccupied." *I'm also not certain how I feel about you being so intimately involved*—I didn't say that. The thought was there.

King Theodore nodded. "This is monumental. I'll be anxious to learn the result." He pulled gloves from his pocket and began to slip them over his hands. "I was headed to the gardens. There's a chill outside, but walking the paths helps me think. Would you like to join me?"

I looked down at my suit coat, wishing I'd dressed warmer. "Yes, sir."

The skies above were dark with translucent clouds. A crescent moon hung low to the horizon. The cool air bit at my cheeks, and my breath materialized as small crystals suspended in the air as I pushed my hands down into the pockets of my suit coat. "Inessa Volkov."

The king nodded.

"I didn't know that she and Roman had a relationship."

"Rumors."

"No, sir. More than rumors."

"Are you sure?" he asked.

I nodded. "Just today, Isabella informed Lucille of

my infidelity. The princess confronted me and showed me a photograph from a Norwegian tabloid."

The king mumbled under his breath. Turning toward me, he said, "If I'd known, you would have been informed. I'm not sure what else Roman kept from us." He shook his head. "We should have brought you on sooner. Who knows the damage he created?"

Though I'd been keeping pace with the king, I stopped my steps, taking in what he'd just said.

Brought me on sooner?

As if I were an understudy waiting in the wings.

"Your Grace, I don't understand how Mrs. Drake found me, chose me, or decided it was acceptable to replace your son."

"She found you. Your role was my decision." King Theodore turned. "We're all replaceable. I told you that early on. We are all replacements. I'm Theodore the second. My grandfather was Theodore the first. My father was Arthur the sixth."

"Yes, but I'm not Roman the second." Or third or fourth.

"No, you're Roman Archibald Godfrey. Upon coronation you may choose another name."

"You are all right with an impostor taking the throne?"

"Until your son is ready. The alternative would land Francis as king consort. That's unacceptable. My plan is to be around long enough to coach you and your son—better than I did in the past. Time is a formidable teacher."

"Your health is good?"

"Much improved." He looked up at the sky. "My work isn't done. I have my next heir to meet."

"Where is Roman?" I asked.

"I'm looking at him." The king stepped closer, lowering his voice. "What is it you want, my son? More money? More power? Lucille? Inessa? You're a stark improvement, and you've committed to Molave. What will make you happy?"

"Neither Lucille nor Inessa is yours to grant."

"You're attracted to Lucille. I see it. Anne sees it. I don't know what Roman told the princess of Borinkia, but it's alarming to consider that they were close. It's dangerous."

"What could he have told her?" I asked.

"Any affairs of state."

Or that he was a replacement, an impostor like me.

"Do you want me to meet with her?" I asked.

"It must be covert."

"Unlike last time."

He shook his head. "A photograph, you say. I want to see it."

I pulled the pages from the inside pocket of my suit coat and handed them to the king.

He took one look and cursed under his breath. "This publication is rubbish. No wonder it wasn't on the crown's radar." He handed the pages back to me. "You have to fix this."

"Lucille," I said as I tucked the pages into my inside pocket.

"What about her?"

"I want her. I want our marriage blessed. She deserves that much, at the very least."

The king nodded. "Isabella told Lucille what you'd done?"

"The infidelity? Yes, sir. The princess was upset as she should be."

"Dinner's cancellation was due to more than being tired, I assume."

"Yes, she's distraught."

"Did you deny it?"

"It was difficult to deny with photographic evidence. I improvised. I told her that Inessa means nothing. Lucille couldn't read the article."

"From the caption that rag put under the picture, Lucille's inability to read Norwegian is a blessing."

The caption speculated on the future pairing of Roman and Inessa, a deal of sorts.

"The people know about your indiscretion," the king said with a hum. "The blessing will be a formal gesture to recommit yourself to Lucille." He inhaled.

"Yes, this will work. Once the blessing is complete, she's yours. Treat her better than Roman did."

"I promise I will."

It felt as if I'd just asked Lucille's father for her hand. In a way, I had. Instead of her father, I'd asked her father-in-law. This was an increasingly fucked-up situation, and somehow, the king's blessing and that of the Church of Molave felt like perhaps there would be one right in our sea of wrongs.

King Theodore resumed walking. "You're a quick study, Roman. We can meet virtually between now and the summit and work out any concerns. I appreciated your commitment to our relationship with the US. I was also pleased by your performance at the banquet. There was never a question as to your identity. Sir Connery informed me that the people were delighted to see the princess with the royal family order."

"Had Roman been against her receiving the honor?"

"Yes. Now that I know about Inessa, it makes sense. I worry that there are other bombshells I didn't know existed."

Me too.

"Francis," I began.

"We never should have allowed him to retain his duchy. I knew his connection to Wilmington was a problem." The king turned to me. "You don't know the history."

I'd studied more history in the last three months than my entire thirty-eight years, yet King Theodore was right. I hadn't studied the Wilmington province. "Educate me."

King Theodore nodded his approval. "Before the Volkovs took over Letanonia, the province of Wilmington was at odds with Letanonia."

"I wasn't aware."

"Despite Norway's resistance to formally recognize Borinkia, there was speculation that Borinkia succeeded due in part to help from the nobles of Wilmington."

"That was decades ago."

"Isabella said the same thing."

"Do you think Francis could be of help connecting me to Inessa?" I asked. "Obviously, Roman was doing it secretly. Did he have a different phone?"

"Francis is probably your best bet. Be careful, Roman. This won't be like dealing with situations you're able to study. We have nothing on this relationship. There's no secret phone that I'm aware of. The ministry guards have searched. I had hoped Roman had left something of record."

"You could ask him?"

"No, I can't."

Despite the cold air, my skin warmed and my stomach twisted.

The king just gave me the information I didn't want to know. In accepting this role, I'd agreed to be Roman Archibald Godfrey for a lifetime, the length of which would be determined by my success.

"See what you can learn from Francis," the king said. "That boy likes to hear himself speak. Just remember, you are Roman Godfrey, the heir to Molave's throne."

"I will, sir."

CHAPTER 24

Lucille

We had been gone from Monovia for only a week, yet as Annabella Castle came into view, I had the sensation of being home in a way that was new and welcomed.

Home.

It was a word I associated with my parents' dwelling in New York City and a word that meant security and familiarity. Home was something I dreamed of having one day with my husband—until the dream died.

Peering through the car windows, I took in the large snow-covered structure, seeing it as I hadn't before. Over the years, this castle had become my prison. I was locked in solitary confinement with every comfort I could want, sans true companionship.

Lady Buckingham, who was seated at my side, had been my greatest confidant and despite her efforts, I was horribly lonely. Yesterday, when Roman mentioned leaving Molave Palace and returning to our home, for the first time, I was happy.

Anxious even.

Yet even when thinking happy thoughts, the awful memory of the picture of Roman and Inessa would ambush me, infiltrating my thoughts. Dropping my chin, I closed my eyes.

Lady Buckingham placed her hand over mine. "Princess, I'm here."

My mistress knew of Roman's infidelity. It was too much for me to keep that a secret from her. She claimed she hadn't known until I showed her the article. Hugging me, she promised to do whatever was possible to help me. As I'd said to Isabella, I told my mistress that I wanted to work on my marriage. Roman's talk of divorce fueled my desire to become relevant to the crown. The news of his affair put us in the spotlight.

With my new Roman at my side, I believed we could be better and stronger than we ever were.

The car ahead of ours stopped. Roman and Lord Martin emerged, being greeted by the castle staff. Once our car proceeded to the covered driveway, the guards opened our door, allowing Lady Buckingham and me to get out.

"Your Highness."

"Welcome back, Your Highness."

I nodded, acknowledging the salutations. Through the first set of doors, the temperature rose. Through the second set of doors, I inhaled, breathing in the warm air as I looked around the foyer. Roman and Lord Martin were already gone. The grand staircase was exactly as it had been. The marble floor and glistening chandelier were unchanged.

And still, it felt different.

"Your coat, ma'am," Geoffrey said as he helped me. "Would you like some tea to warm you?"

"Yes, Geoffrey. I'll take it in my office."

Lady Buckingham walked at my side until we reached my office. The room was bigger than my private office in our apartments in Molave Palace, yet most of my staff was back in Molave City. They had a larger office suite on the main floor of the palace.

"If I may," she said as we entered the office.

"Go on."

"Lady Larsen called about the news."

"The news?" I questioned.

"Ma'am, I had to inform her about...the prince."

My eyes closed. "I don't want to think about it."

"She'd like to speak to you. While the news wasn't prominent in Molave, she's discovered it was in Norway and the States."

The States.

"My parents." My eyes opened wider. "My father. He asked if I was happy. He must have known."

Lady Buckingham nodded.

"No wonder Dame Robinson said what she did."

"And what was that?"

I shook my head. "It doesn't matter."

"Lady Larsen believes it does. She thinks you should make a statement."

"No," I said. "My statement is standing beside the prince. It's him standing beside me as he did in Brynad. I won't further rumors or verify that rubbish with a statement."

"Perhaps you should discuss it with the prince?"

"We have. I won't waste any more time on the subject. The prince and I decided upon the two cities to visit next week before the summit. I'll call Lady Larsen to be sure she's coordinating with Roman's office and the royal guards."

Geoffrey entered with a tray and my tea.

"Your Highness," he said with a bow before setting down the tray.

"Please alert the kitchen that I'd like my midday meal."

"What would you like, ma'am?"

"Soup and a sandwich." I looked to Lady Buckingham. "Apparently, making my own decisions makes me hungry."

"I'll see to your meal," she said.

Alone with my hot tea, I called Lady Larsen. We were discussing the cities of Odnessa and Forthwith when Lady Buckingham entered with my lunch. Something about her expression, her pinched forehead and pursed lips, caused the small hairs on the back of my neck to stand to attention.

"Lady Larsen," I said into the telephone, "please be sure everything is set and coordinated with the prince's staff."

"Yes, ma'am."

"Goodbye." I hung up the receiver. "What is wrong?" I asked Lady Buckingham.

"Mrs. Templeton informed me that the ministry guards visited here again on the day of banquet. She said they insisted on searching your and the prince's apartments."

"What do they expect to find?"

"I don't know. The prince is angered. He's up in the apartments now."

I stood. "Angered?"

"Perhaps, ma'am, you should wait until he calms to check your private suite."

"They entered our private suites? Our bedchambers?"

"Yes."

My appetite disappeared as I turned toward the doorway. "I need to go upstairs."

She reached for my hand. "I've been told he's very upset. It would be better..."

I stood taller. "If I'm going to make my marriage work, it won't be by cowering."

"I'll go with you."

"No. Take my meal back to the kitchen to keep it warm." I looked out the open doorway and sighed. "I'm going upstairs."

My pulse thumped in double time as I climbed the grand staircase. Roman's voice came into range as I neared our apartments. I couldn't make out each word, only the harshness of his tone and level of volume. Three months ago, I might have turned around.

This wasn't three months ago.

Now we're a team.

Entering our connecting parlor, I stared at the room of people.

"Your Highness," they all said with a bow or curtsy. Their main attention was focused on the open door to my husband's suite.

Without a word or acknowledgment, I hurried back to my bedchamber. Nothing appeared out of place. I opened drawers and threw open the cupboard. Hurriedly, I went back out and entered Roman's side.

The front parlor was unchanged. I went down the

hallway to his bedchamber. At the sight of me, Roman's shouting ceased, yet his face and neck were reddened as the man before his would be.

"Your Highness," I said with a curtsy. "Leave us," I demanded of Lord Martin. "And take everyone with you."

Lord Martin looked at Roman who finally spoke, "You heard the princess. Go."

As Lord Martin closed the door, I looked around. Books were pulled from his bookcases. Some were strewn about while others were stacked.

"Did they find it—the secret room?" I asked.

"This is an invasion of our privacy."

I started lifting books and placing them back in the bookcase. "I'm surprised they left such a mess."

"They didn't. I did. As soon as I walked in, I saw the books were out of place."

"Out of place?" I asked.

Roman closed his eyes and inhaled. "I like details."

"Okay?"

"Apparently, so did Roman or Noah. The books were shelved in alphabetical order. I noticed that the first night I was here at Annabella. It wasn't obvious, but the fact that had changed meant we'd been searched again."

"Have you looked?"

He shook his head. "No, I couldn't with everyone present."

"Instead, you screamed like a raving maniac?"

"Maybe Roman had cause for some of his madness."

I opened my eyes wide. "If anyone doubted your behavior as authentic, you've now convinced them that you are Roman."

"Go check." He lifted his chin to the door. "Be sure we're alone."

"Yes, Your Highness."

As I started to walk toward the door, Roman reached for my hand. "Never fear me, my princess. I will act in any manner necessary to keep us from harm."

My cheeks lifted in a smile. "I trust you." I kissed his cheek.

Down the hallway I searched Roman's private office, his study, and his parlor. Twisting the lock on the main doors to the connecting parlor, I locked us inside. When I re-entered his bedchamber, I confirmed we were alone.

Roman reached under the third shelf from the floor in the second bookcase to the left and stepped back. The bookcase moved back into the secret room before swiveling. Cool air, much as the opening of a refrigerator, came from the room.

"What if it's all gone?" I asked.

"Our lives just got harder."

I reached for his hand. "If they found it, that doesn't mean we knew about it."

He activated the flashlight on his cellphone.

Together we stepped inside.

CHAPTER 25

Roman

I let out the breath I was holding as the flashlight app's beam illuminated the narrow room. The bookcase was as I'd left it, and rubber tubs still lined the one wall. There was one exception to the room being as we originally found it. The journal we'd been reading was stuffed over the books, not shelved as we'd originally found it.

"Thank goodness," Lucille whispered, her grasp of my hand loosening.

"This is dangerous." I turned, meeting Lucille's blue orbs. "We need to move it."

"It? All of it? How?" She turned a full circle. "There's too much. Besides, they've searched three times. They must be ready to give up."

"The king is scared. He's afraid that Roman's relationship with Inessa is the tip of the iceberg." I motioned toward the opening. "The ministry guards were so fucking close."

"Do you think they found it and left it?"

Roman shook his head. "No. If they'd found this, the entire room would be cleared out." I led Lucille back to the bedchamber. "You know this castle better than I. Where can we hide all the things, maybe somewhere they've already searched."

"There isn't a place, not one I know of. The staff would notice us carrying books, boxes, and tubs. Thus far, Mrs. Templeton and the others have been able to answer honestly that they know nothing about any of this. I don't want to involve them." She looked back to the darkened space. "Nothing incriminates us. It's all Noah. I think we should tell King Theo we found it."

"No." I pressed the lever and stepped back as the bookcase closed.

"Roman, this is Noah's fault. Inessa is Noah's fault. My last five years of hell were his fault. Why can't we give the king more reasons to convict him."

"Convict him? Should I be convicted for taking a job?"

"You know that's not what I mean. Noah shouldn't be convicted for taking a job but for harming Molave."

I took Lucille's hand. "Noah is dead, my princess."

Her hands trembled in my grasp as the color drained from her cheeks.

"I haven't officially been told that news, but I know it to be true. I asked the king to talk to Roman, to learn if there were other bombshells we should know about.

He said he couldn't. Not that he wouldn't, but he couldn't."

Letting go of my hand, Lucille wrapped her arms around her midsection and walked to my bed. Slowly, she sank to the side of the mattress.

In two strides I was at her side, crouching down by her feet. "This is life and death, my princess. My agent and now Noah. Noah told us in the first journal that if we found his writings, he would have failed and been replaced."

"Where is Roman? The real one," she asked.

"We won't stop until we learn the answer to that question."

Sniffling, Lucille lifted her chin. "I've been so mad at Roman—Noah—since learning what he did. I've regretted every time I submitted to him, pacified him, ignored the glaring large neon signs that told me he didn't love me. I've been fantasizing about confronting him." She grinned. "You know, like the show where the wife feeds her husband to the dogs."

"Remind me not to get on your bad side."

Her smile dimmed. "I feel badly. He wasn't born to this. He agreed and decided he hated the life. His only hope was…"

My eyes met hers.

"His only hope," I said, "was to become king or to undermine the king and monarchy with Borinkia."

"I don't know what to think."

I stood and paced by the bookcase, avoiding the strewn books. "I have the sinking feeling that working with Prince Alek and getting involved with Princess Inessa weren't Noah's only crimes."

I looked around the room. "Will you help me shelve the books?"

"Alphabetical? Seriously?"

"Yes, it was the only way you could get me to calm down."

"Tonight, we need to read more," she said.

"I agree. I want to find out if there's information about how Roman and Francis communicated. Remember, I said that Francis told me I'd been ignoring his messages. I haven't received any messages. He also said Inessa was upset I hadn't contacted her. There are no phone records of Roman contacting the princess of Borinkia."

"A secret phone?"

"I asked the king. He didn't know of one." I shrugged. "It makes the most sense."

"I think," Lucille said, reaching for my hand, "after traveling and this invasion of our privacy, I will be retiring early tonight."

My kiss landed on her forehead. "Good plan, my princess." I stood tall. "Look at me, Lucille."

Her chin rose as her blue orbs stared into mine.

"I need a promise from you."

"What promise?"

"You won't open the room without me."

"Will you promise the same?" she asked.

I hadn't planned on it, but she was right. If we were a team, we needed to learn as a team. "I promise."

"Then I shall, too. Send for me tonight. Lady Buckingham will leave earlier."

"I'd like to spend the night as we have been, not reading journals and looking through totes."

Lucille's eyes shone. "Your Highness."

A short time later, when Lord Martin met me outside our apartments, his lips were pressed together in a straight line.

"Say what's on your mind."

"I'll send a butler into your bedchamber to clean the mess."

"There's no mess," I said.

"Sir, you wouldn't clean..."

"I didn't. The princess did. She has an uncanny knack for smoothing rough waters."

He spoke softly. "You were overdue for a tirade. It was very convincing."

"Do you have any idea what the ministry guards are searching to find?" I asked.

"No, sir. I can only assume it is something from Roman, the one before you."

I nodded. "Perhaps you could reach out to Lord Avery."

"He's retired, sir."

"And he's unreachable?"

"Yes."

"Why would you accept the position to help me? This is dangerous."

"I am loyal to Molave and to the Godfreys. You are our hope. I have faith that you'll succeed."

"Inform the kitchen that the princess and I will have our evening meal early in our apartments. The travel, the search, and the recent news" —yes, Lord Martin was informed by me about Inessa— "have tired the princess."

"Yes, Your Highness."

Later, as I sat across the table from Lucille, I took in her appearance. She'd been beautiful as we traveled, in slacks and a jumper. At that time, her long hair had been tethered back into a low ponytail. Now, she was gorgeous in a light-pink dress with a long jacket and heels.

"You're stunning, as ever," I said softly. "You do not need to dress up when it is only us."

Pink came to her cheeks. "Lady Buckingham suggested the change of clothes, to aid in the repair of our marriage."

My smile quirked. "Tell Lady Buckingham I prefer

you without clothes. That is how I'd like you to come to dinner." Her cheeks grew rosier. "Breakfast and lunch."

"I will not tell my mistress anything of the kind."

She smiled. "Will I be able to tell her it worked?"

"You said you wouldn't tell her my wishes."

"I won't. Those are for my ears only. I'll inform her that you've requested me tonight. I'm already bathed, so I should be available when you call."

"I will call."

CHAPTER 26

Lucille

Approaching Roman's bedchamber, my sense of anticipation was different than it had been in the past. It wasn't lovemaking that would occupy our night; it was learning more from the secret room. Without knocking, I turned the large knob and pushed the door inward.

The motion was such a simple, menial task, and yet it brought me immense joy. Never in all our years of marriage had Roman and I had the level of comfort with one another that we shared today. It was difficult for my mind to separate the men, yet something as mundane as stepping into Roman's private bedchamber unannounced highlighted the stark contrast.

As the whole of his bedchamber came into view, I saw Roman was seated in a plush chair across the room, sitting back with his ankle over his knee.

"Princess," Roman said with a smile as he looked up from what he was reading.

The navy-blue satin of his pajamas reflected the light from his reading lamp. His dark hair was damp and combed back. From across the distance, I was struck with how strikingly handsome he was. I'd always thought Roman was attractive, but now his splendor was more than simply his outward appearance. There was a beauty innate to *this* Roman that came from within.

Flames roared within his fireplace, casting the entire bedchamber in a warm orange glow. Laying his book, opened to the page he was reading, upside down on a table, Roman stood to greet me.

"Your Highness." Warmth circulated beneath my skin at the way Roman looked at me, the shimmer in his smile and the intensity of his stare. As his dark eyes scanned from my hair to my toes, my heart fluttered and my core twisted. Although my long satin dressing gown covered a thigh-length pale-blue nightgown with lace straps and trim, it seemed as if with only his gaze, Roman was stripping me bare, seeing beneath each layer.

In a few strides, the prince met me, wrapping his arm around my waist and pulling me to him. His pajamas did little to hide the hardness of his toned, muscular body as I melded against him.

Our lips found one another's, and our kiss deepened. Toothpaste and the fresh scent of bodywash filled my senses as I lifted my hands to his wide shoulders.

When our kiss ended, Roman tipped his forehead to mine. "I could do that all night long."

His deep baritone tenor rumbled through me as I nodded. "I wish we could. I'm nervous about what we may learn."

"We need to learn."

Swallowing, I nodded again.

His attention went to my feet as a smile lifted his cheeks. "The secret room is chilly. Do you not have slippers?"

"Lady Buckingham would have questioned." I tilted my head. "She knows I prefer bare feet to slippers. I get tired of the high heels."

Shaking his head, Roman went to the chest of drawers and came back with a pair of his socks. "Put these on. They'll keep you from freezing."

I giggled as I took the pair. "You would never think to offer these."

"They're only socks."

I held them to my chest. "Yes, but they're yours."

"I recall offering you my jacket one cool, rainy night in the gardens."

The memories of that night came back. "It was when you confessed your identity." I smiled. "It was when I thought I'd created you, wished for you. You were my dream come true."

"I couldn't conjure you in a dream." Roman gently reached for my chin and lifted my face upward. "I have fallen in love with you, Lucille. I'd prefer not to lose you to the common cold."

"Socks won't stop a cold. It's a virus—"

His finger covered my lips. "As your prince, I command you to put on the socks."

"Yes, Your Highness."

"I'm going to go lock the door to the connecting parlor."

As I sat in the chair where Roman had been sitting, I donned the too-large socks and picked up the book he'd been reading. I couldn't read the title.

"What language is this?" I asked when he returned.

"Estonian. It's a Finnic language."

"And you can read it?"

"Yes, and I can speak it." He tilted his head. "Not with a Molavian accent. I'd need to work on that."

"And you also speak and read Norwegian?"

"Yes."

"Why?" I tried to explain. "I don't mean that to sound demeaning. Your abilities are amazing, but most Americans are awful at languages. That's one of the reasons we—as a whole—got the nickname of the ugly American."

Roman sighed. "I moved around a lot as a child. My mother was stationed all around Europe and the world."

"Stationed?"

"She was an airman first class."

"That's a fascinating job." My smile faded. "Doesn't she miss you?"

"She passed away over ten years ago."

"I'm sorry," I said. Realizing my failure, I added, "I'm also sorry I never thought to ask about your family."

Roman shook his head. "Not much to ask about. I have two sisters. We usually call on birthdays, and that's about it. We've gone our separate ways."

"What about your father?"

"My mother didn't marry him. I know his name because it's on my birth certificate. He was around when I was very young, a fellow air force officer. After that, he never reached out to me, so I never thought of reaching out to him."

I went to Roman and laid my hand on his arm. "I'm sorry if this conversation makes you sad."

He shook his head. "Princess, I am an open book to you. Talking about what was my family doesn't make me sad. My mom was great. I have good memories, and my life as a child and teen was an adventure. That could possibly be why I chose the career path I did. Those earlier years gave me confidence. My stepdad was cool. He never treated me different than the girls. I guess I just never felt that connected."

"You met my father," I said. "I want you to meet my mother. She's a fabulous person."

"Does she think I'm an arrogant ass as your father does?"

"Pompous ass," I corrected. "My mom, as you probably know, was born a baroness in Letanonia. She was rightfully concerned about me marrying into royalty, especially given Molave's geographic proximity to Borinkia. As for you, she will love you...*you*. All she cares about is my happiness." I sighed. "Lady Larsen said the news of your relationship with Princess Inessa was everywhere in the States."

"Fuck, I'm sorry."

I shook my head. "I think it's why my father asked if I wanted a divorce. I think he knew but didn't want to tell me. He wanted me to know I had an alternative." I reached for Roman's hand and spun the wedding ring on his fourth finger. "You make me happy. My mom will see that."

"I want you happy, Lucille. I also want you safe. I know we promised to only open the room together, but I think it might be better if you're not involved. No one knows you know the truth about me. Whatever is in there could be dangerous knowledge."

"You promised me, my prince. I'm scared, but you also promised me that I never needed to fear you and when I was frightened, you would be at my side."

"It sounds like I promise many things."

"You do," I said, "and I trust you, not only with my body but also with my heart. Is that trust misplaced?"

"No." His gaze intensified. "I don't want you hurt."

"I've been hurt, Roman. I need to know why."

He took a deep breath. "Ready?"

"Yes."

I waited as Roman walked to the bookcase and activated the lever. Just like the times before, the second bookcase on the left moved back and swiveled inward. Remembering where the light switch was, I walked past him.

Goosebumps materialized under my dressing gown as the cooler air surrounded me. Even with Roman's socks, the floor was cold. Pushing the switch upward, the narrow room filled with light.

"Where should we begin?" I asked.

CHAPTER 27

Roman

Going to the bookcase at the far wall, I lifted the journal we'd already skimmed. "This journal is from five years ago, when Noah first became Roman." I looked through the rows of what I assumed were all journals and ran my finger over the spines. While colors and sizes varied, not one had any exterior marking. I reached for the last book on the lowest shelf. After a brief glance over my shoulder, I opened the front page. "This first entry is dated this past June." I looked up at Lucille. "I think we can assume the journals proceed in chronological order."

Lucille's unsettled state of mind showed in her body language. If she too were an actor, she'd perfected the skill of wordlessly portraying intense emotion. Fear of the unknown emanated from her pores. She used her arms as a shield, wrapping them around her midsection. Concern was visible in the way her forehead wrinkled, her eyebrows knitted together, and her lips pressed together in a straight line.

Standing, I stepped toward her.

Face-to-face, I surrounded her trembling body with my embrace. "You don't have to help me." I leaned back, looking down to her beautiful face. "I can tell that this upsets you."

Lucille nodded. "It does, but that doesn't mean I can ignore it. Obviously, I've ignored or been blind to too much."

Within my grasp, her posture straightened, as if she were gaining strength before my eyes.

Her voice came forth resolute and strong. "I need to do this. I want to understand."

After brushing my lips on her forehead, I nodded. "You're not alone, Lucille. Remember that."

A smile curled her lips. "Sometimes I still believe you're here as an answer to my prayers."

"My presence has less to do with divine intervention and more to do with royal manipulation." I tilted my head toward the bookcase. "Despite how horrible of a husband Noah was to you, those journals could open our eyes to what manipulation was done by him and to him. For that, I'm grateful."

Lucille shook her head. "I'm not grateful for Noah. I married Roman Godfrey. What became of him?"

Taking a step back, I replied, "I don't know. Maybe the answer is in there. Are you sure you're up to this?"

"Yes."

"Okay, we could make quicker progress if instead of reading together, one of us starts at the beginning and the other one in the last journal he wrote." I reached for the last journal I'd opened and turned to the princess. "Is that all right with you?"

"What about these totes?" She gestured toward the stacked plastic containers. "You said it sounded as if Roman and Francis were in secret communication as well as Roman and Inessa. Do you think we should go through the totes to search for a phone?"

"Why don't you start with the totes," I suggested. "You would recognize the contents better than I."

Lucille nodded. "In here or out in the bedchamber?"

Noticing the way Lucille's hands trembled, I replied, "It's cold in here. I'll carry a few totes to the bedchamber and then come out with some journals."

"We have to be sure everything is back by morning."

Lifting the top tote, I answered, "That we do."

After carrying two of the large totes and a stack of the most recent journals into my bedchamber, I closed the bookcase, blocking the chill. With the fire still roaring in the hearth, Lucille and I settled on the rug before the hearth, basking in the warmth the flames offered.

"This is so odd," she said, peering down into the first tote.

"What?"

She pulled a duffel bag from the tote. Inside was packed with clothes. Warm jumpers, blue jeans, and even hiking boots. Her blue orbs found mine. "Roman never wore casual clothes. Never."

"Do you think they're his?"

Reading the tags within, she nodded. "They would fit him. Why would he have clothes he'd never wear?"

"In a duffel bag? It was to escape," I said. "To fit into the crowd and disappear."

Lucille's lips pursed. "Do you think that's what he did? He escaped?"

"I think that was his plan." Looking at the duffel bag, I added, "I'm not sure his plan succeeded."

"Let me keep looking," she said, digging deeper into the tote.

I opened the journal that began June of this year. It was only two months before the Firm contacted Andrew with their offer. I was living the life of an esteemed warlord, dating Rita, and blissfully unaware of a country named Molave.

Noah – 5 months ago

My anxiety is getting worse. They're all out to get me. I don't know who I can trust anymore. I feel my nerves constantly surrounding me, strangling me. My skin is tight, too tight. I'm trapped and nothing I do will help me. Locked in this life that isn't mine, I long for the life I left behind.

If I don't break free soon, I will go mad.

It's as if over the past five years I've transformed into another person.

Noah.

Noah.

Noah.

I write my name to remember it. No one ever says it, as if I am cursed—the real me.

I am.

When this job started, I believed I could do it. Now every aspect of Roman's life is infuriating. I'm dreading our upcoming tour. The king has warned me that it must be well received. That alone is reason to fail.

My only relief comes with the medications Lord Avery provides. I've stopped thinking about things in the realm of right versus wrong. No longer do I care about the side effects of the steroids as long as they do what I want them to do. Despite the king's urging, I will continue to do anything in my power to not impregnate Lucille.

If someone else is reading this, heed my warning: do not bring an innocent human into this farce. The meds Lord Avery provides help to decrease sperm count. The other side effects are hell, but again, worth it. I've also gotten into the habit of masturbating before Lucille comes to me. Get those fast swimmers out.

While I used to take the capsules sparingly, lately, I need more.

* * *

Shaking my head, I let the words on the page soak in.

"Princess," I said, looking over to where she sat. Her long hair hung over her shoulders as she looked down, surrounded by a strange assortment of odds and ends.

"Did you learn something?" she asked, making eye contact.

Damn, seeing her sitting there, my heart ached for what she'd been through.

"Should I read it?"

I shook my head, turning the page. "No, I want you to know, your inability to conceive wasn't your fault."

Her forehead furrowed. "Why? What did you read?"

"He didn't want you to get pregnant. I believe he was taking steroids to lower his sperm count."

"No. Mr. Davies wouldn't approve that."

"I don't think they came through the physician."

Lucille's shoulders drooped. "He would continually demean me, saying how I'd failed at my one job."

Leaving the journal, I crawled toward her. Fist, knee, fist, knee. As I moved closer, her smile returned.

"What are you doing?" she asked.

"I'm stalking you, my princess." In a few more strides, I was close enough to kiss her. As I did, I pushed forward, until Lucille's head was on the soft rug and her blue eyes were staring up at me. "You are not and never have been a failure."

Her expression sobered. "I want to read it."

I shook my head. "Trust me."

"Have you read anything about Inessa?"

"No, not yet. I do think he was trying to upset the king. It could be why he performed poorly on the world stage during your tour. I get the feeling he felt trapped." I shrugged. "Okay, it's not a feeling. That's what the journal said."

"Let me show you something."

Nodding, I moved back, allowing Lucille to sit up. She reached for a leather bag, reminding me of a travel shaving kit I once had. Unzipping the top, she opened the bag.

"What is it?" I asked.

"I didn't know, but maybe it's what you were talking about."

I took the bag from her and looked inside. There were small containers of red and white capsules, blue tablets, and pink tablets. I sucked in a breath at the glass vials and multiple syringes.

"Do you think those are the steroids?" Lucille asked.

"I don't know much about this, but from what I can remember, steroids can be taken to cause muscle growth. It's why some actors use it."

"Have you?"

"No, Princess, I went about muscle growth the old-fashioned way. I worked out." Looking into the bag, I shook my head. "I knew a guy..." I met her gaze. "This stuff can be addicting."

"It didn't give him muscles," Lucille said. "Not like yours."

"What about other substances? Did he drink a lot of alcohol or smoke?"

"No smoking." She shrugged. "I honestly avoided him after dinner when possible. I don't know how much or what he drank. He always had wine with dinner."

"Look at me, Princess."

The innocence in her gaze as she obeyed made me want to reach through the pages and knock sense into the man who'd hurt her. "I'll do some research, but I think this could tell us a lot about Noah's state of mind and decisions he made."

Lucille stood and walked to the second tote. Lifting the lid, she smiled. "Roman, I found your means of communication."

CHAPTER 28

Lucille

I pressed the button on the side of the cell phone. The screen remained black. "It's dead."

Roman searched through the second tote, finding a cord and charger. "First things first, we need to charge it." He also pulled out a tablet. "I'm going to assume he had VPNs to keep these hidden from the Firm."

"This is good, right?"

"As long as he used a virtual network and charging these doesn't send some signal to the Firm, I'd say it's good."

Sitting back on the soft rug, I watched as Roman plugged in the phone and tablet. Next, he reached again for the journal.

"Do you speak Russian?"

His dark gaze came my way. "Not well, but yes. It has similarities to Finnic languages. Why do you ask?"

"The Volkovs are of Russian descent. When they invaded Letanonia, turning it into Borinkia, they chose

Russian as the national language. To speak to Inessa, you would need to speak in Russian."

"Was Roman—Noah, I mean—able to speak multiple languages?"

"Yes, I think."

"You think?"

"I only heard him speak in English and Norwegian. The king is capable."

"Damn," Roman said, "I wish I could call Dustin."

"Your voice coach?"

Roman nodded. "The king wants me to secretly contact Alek. I'll ask the king about the languages."

"He wants you to contact him. My father made it clear that there can be no relationship between Molave and Borinkia if Molave is to continue its relationship with the US."

"I know. It's complicated, but we need to learn what Noah did. From what little I've read, I think he was purposely trying to harm Molave."

Standing, I stretched my legs and turned a complete circle. "Is there any reason to keep any of this stuff out?"

"No." Roman scoffed. "I'm not taking his drugs."

A smile curled my lips. "You don't need to build muscle, Your Highness."

"I'm glad you approve."

"I do and I'm tired," I admitted. "I'll put everything

except the phone and tablet back, and I should go to my bedchamber to sleep."

"You don't need to leave. Sleep here. I'll turn the lights down while I read."

The only private interaction the old Roman and I had was sex. Once we were done, I would leave or he would. The idea of simply sleeping beside the man I loved more each and every day was comforting.

"I'd like that."

As Roman carried the totes back into the secret room, I looked within for an outlet. "Maybe," I said, finding one, "it would be better to charge the phone and tablet within the room. I'd hate for us to forget they're out there and Lord Martin or Lady Caroline find them."

Roman nodded. "I trust them, but I also don't want to put them in a difficult or dangerous situation."

Stifling a yawn, I agreed.

Roman reached for my hand. "Come, my princess. Let's put you to bed."

Taking off my dressing gown, I sat on the edge of Roman's bed and removed his socks. "Thank you." Warmth circulated through me as I handed him the socks. While he didn't say a word as he took them, I saw his exchange. The sensation that I was cared for and loved in the way he looked at me filled me with warmth. Truly, it was addicting. I could bask under the glow of his dark stare for the rest of my life.

Addicting.

Could Noah's addiction have affected his personality?

Lying back, I pulled the blankets over me as the room grew dimmer. With only the illumination from the fire and a small lamp on Roman's side of the bed, he joined me. The mattress dipped seconds before his warmth radiated beneath the covers. Turning on my side, I curled next to him. "If you learn anything important, will you tell me?" I asked, looking up past his now-bare chest up to his handsome face.

"Yes. We're a team." His lips kissed the top of my head.

"You could read aloud."

"Okay."

His deep baritone tenor filled the air. Closing my eyes, I expected concentrating to be difficult. My thoughts were filled with the steroids, my inability to conceive, and the clothes packed for a quick getaway. Yet as Roman read, all thoughts other than his words faded.

Noah – 5 months ago (a day after the last entry I'd read)

I spoke with Senator Sutton today. He's a conde-

scending piece of shit if you ask me. I refused to settle for a repeat of our last deal. I don't care if it upsets the relationship with the US. The damn baroness is in his ear and head. Her influence is evident. It's no wonder Lucille continues to push to do more for the country. I'm sick and tired of the same conversation.

I can't be the one to walk away from the US deal—the king would never approve. But if I push hard enough, I believe the senator will. It's his damn allegiance to his daughter that keeps him holding on. That allegiance won't pacify his fellow senators or his constituents. Besides, I've been thinking about the deal Francis proposed.

Who knew he was as unhappy with the Godfreys as I?

Yeah, he loves his wife and kids, but he's had it with the restrictions the king has placed on him. I don't blame him. He's a duke, and the king thinks he should bow to him.

I was on the verge of telling Francis the truth, that I'm not the real Roman, but I couldn't do it. It's not that I give a shit about his safety. It's mine. I swore to maintain the façade. I can't negotiate with Borinkia as an impostor. No one can know the truth.

I woke to soft kisses peppering my cheek.

As I blinked away sleep, I puckered my lips, ready for whatever was about to happen. My hands skirted over the wide chest before me as the only light coming from the dying fire illuminated Roman's bedchamber.

"Roman," I said sleepily.

"It's nearly five, my princess. You should go to your bedchamber, or we'll be found."

Stretching my neck and arching my back, I brought my lips to his. "I don't want to leave. I think I sleep better at your side than I have in" —a smile spread across my face— "in many years."

"I don't want you to leave. I want to tug this nightgown over your head and spend the next hour or more buried deep inside you."

"You do not say such things."

Roman's smile quirked. "Oh, Princess, that was my PG version. What I want to say is much more direct."

"That won't make me leave." I ran my palms over his chest, feeling the soft dark hair I knew to be present. Down his tight abs. Lower still.

"Fuck."

"Yes, please, Your Highness."

"You're killing me, Lucille," Roman said, rolling onto his back. "Tomorrow—today," he corrected, "I want to take you on a drive." He turned his head toward me. "I know that's allowed because I read about it."

"It's been a long time. Before we were married, we used to drive all over Molave without guards."

"I'll schedule some time this afternoon. It would do us good to get away."

My stomach twisted. "You want to talk to me alone. Is it something you read?"

"It's me wanting you alone and yes, a few things I read. I want to test the boundaries to see what we can do without the king's admonishment."

I nodded. "Okay, Your Highness. I would never turn you down."

"You can, you know."

My smile returned. "Why would I turn down the opportunity to be alone with the man I love?"

Sitting up, Roman dropped his forehead to mine. "I love you too. We will figure this out."

CHAPTER 29

Roman

Securing the automobile was easier than convincing Lord Martin that I could drive, take Lucille away from Annabella Castle, and do it all without royal guards.

"How did you learn of this privilege?" Lord Martin asked as he accompanied me toward my offices.

"Lucille," I replied sharply, stating the untruth. "The king told me to work on our marriage. She mentioned that we used to have more time alone."

Lord Martin's eyebrows furrowed. "Princess Lucille..."

"On with it."

"Sir," he spoke low as we traversed mostly empty corridors. There were much fewer people at Annabella Castle than Molave Palace. "You appear as the prince when fully clothed. If you take this further—intimately—she will know. I mean, anyone can see."

"I've mentioned that I've been exercising."

"If I may."

Closing my eyes, I exhaled. "What?"

"The princess has always been a concern. Perhaps the king is wrong. Working on a marriage that isn't yours is beyond what you were hired to do."

Stopping in the middle of a first-floor hallway, I turned to my assistant. My voice was lowered to a growl. "Do not speak to me as if I'm not the prince. Do you understand?"

Bowing his head, Lord Martin acquiesced.

"Perhaps another time would be better for a drive," he suggested. "The frigid temperature is a concern."

Ignoring Lord Martin's advice, I resumed walking. "Today, I'll work from my office until midday meal. Have the cook pack a picnic." The thought had just occurred to me. "I like that idea. The princess and I will return before nightfall."

"Sir, a picnic?" He shook his head. "That isn't you."

"It is me. I can't be expected to fully give up who I am. As the world stands, I am Roman Godfrey, the Prince of Molave, Duke of Monovia. I want to take my wife for a fucking drive. That is what I'll do."

"Sir," he admonished.

"Fuck is a new word in my vocabulary," I said loudly. "Get used to it."

"Yes, sir. I'll go speak to the cook."

Resilient Reign

"And inform Lady Buckingham of the princess's change in schedule."

Monday morning flew by as I fielded calls and video conferences in preparation for the upcoming summit. Once I was alone on a video call with the king, I asked, "I'd like to broach a subject that is better if only the two of us hear. Is that possible on this call?"

King Theodore sat taller as he stared into the camera. "Is this important?"

"Yes, sir. I believe it is."

"Be direct, son."

"If I'm to speak to Inessa in the Russian language, I'll need help."

King Theodore's serious expression morphed as a hearty laugh came from his side of the call. "If you were to speak to her in Russian at all, it would be an issue. Despite tutors for years, you've only mastered Norwegian and English."

"I speak more than two languages."

"Then use your abilities to your advantage. Listen to those around you. People are often willing to say the truth when they believe they're not being understood. As for speaking or writing, you would only communicate in one of two languages."

"I found a book in my bedchamber. It is a recounting of the history regarding Letanonia and Borinkia. It's an interesting perspective written in

Estonian. Why would that book be here if Roman" —I quickly corrected myself— "if *I* couldn't read it?"

The king's brow furrowed. "That's a good question. Have you found any other books, writings, anything?"

"In the office, sir."

He shook his head. "Everything in the office has been vetted. Keep your linguistic abilities to yourself. As I said, use your knowledge of languages to your advantage. Have you contacted Francis regarding what we talked about?"

"Not yet. In two days, the princess and I will travel to Forthwith. I thought it better to speak to him in person."

"Will you be addressing the people in the province?"

"Yes. That's our plan."

"Keep me apprised. I'll see you in person on Friday morning in Oslo."

"Yes, sir."

As I disconnected the call, I battled with the reality I saw and heard with my own eyes compared to what I'd read last night. After Lucille fell asleep, I spent the next three hours reading until the words on the page began to blur.

Despite the first journal being prophetic regarding

Noah's future, the last journal was exceedingly darker. A man trapped in another life with no one except Lord Avery to speak with. No one to verify his true presence. It was obvious that by the time he wrote the entries, he'd stopped caring about Molave, Lucille, or even himself. It was as if he was hell-bent on revenge and destruction.

Revenge for taking his life.

Revenge for assigning him a wife.

Destruction of everything under his influence in retaliation for what he interpreted as being made the king's scapegoat for the Firm's misjudgments.

The tariffs that were in place when I first arrived were a means to upset the Molavian citizens, to cause unrest, and to cast a shadow on the monarchy. The decision was his unilaterally. I needed to go back in time, read more about how Noah began and continued his downward spiral.

To my surprise, there was nothing in the journal entries I'd read regarding Inessa. Alek was mentioned multiple occasions, in regard to a deal. Francis was mentioned, but not the princess of Borinkia. I'd hoped for more information.

Before turning off my computer, using a satellite program, I mapped out the princess's and my afternoon excursion. With the unmarked car, we would be able to drive through cities and villages incognito. I even found a site for our picnic. It was an hour's drive higher into the mountains.

A short time later, I was in my bedchamber looking through my clothes, when I decided Noah had been right. I needed some more casual attire. For a moment, I considered entering the secret room and raiding the duffel bag. Blue jeans and hiking boots would be perfect for what I had planned.

It only took me a few seconds to veto my own idea.

Choosing from the cupboard less-formal clothes than I had been wearing, I began to remove my suit.

"Your Highness," Lord Martin said, entering my private area with barely a knock. "I went to your offices. Here..." He hurried toward me. "Let me help you with that." He held the suitcoat as I pulled my arms from the sleeves. "The cook has a basket packed with the lunch you requested. The car is outside the main entrance."

I met Lord Martin's worried expression.

"Lighten up," I teased. "I feel like I'm going on a date."

The tips of my assistant's lips moved slightly higher. "I didn't work directly with...you in the past. Such as you, I was required to do research."

"Did you talk to Lord Avery?"

"No, sir," he said with a downcast expression. "If I had, he would have known of his impending retirement. Everything was timed to work out seamlessly." He took a deep breath. "I am not in a position to pass judgment."

"Go on."

"The princess deserves better than what she had. I don't know how you can do it, but if you are able to repair what was done, I implore you to remember that knowledge is dangerous. I accepted that danger when I agreed to be your personal assistant. Lady Caroline did the same. Princess Lucille wasn't given that choice. If you would feel the desire to confide in her, you are risking everything—you are risking her."

Nodding, I accepted his advice.

It was true, every word.

I'd already put her in danger.

"Thank you, sir," Lord Martin said. "I'm grateful you allowed me to voice my concern."

"Why would Lady Buckingham look the other way when the princess was treated poorly?"

"It wasn't her choice. We, Lady Buckingham and I, have our positions. Our stations in life. Our influence is narrow. If Mary would have taken her concerns to a higher level, you, Your Highness, would have removed her from her position. She did what she could to help the princess. She cares deeply for her."

Turning, I took in my reflection in the mirror. I was down to the padded shirt and boxer briefs. "I'm going to stop wearing this padded shirt. You're right about my appearance."

"Perhaps, Lady Caroline can get you one more with less padding before you give it up altogether."

"One more," I agreed. As I picked up the trousers from the bed, I added, "Blue jeans. I'd like some more casual attire for outings such as this." When my assistant began to speak, I lifted my hand. "Small changes. I get it. We'll make them work."

"Yes, Your Highness."

CHAPTER 30

Lucille

The interior of the car was filled with warmth as I took my seat at Roman's side. It had been nearly a year since I'd sat in the front seat. It had been that long since I'd been asked to take a ride. During our courtship, Roman would not only take me on secluded drives, but he would take me flying in his glider.

Roman's hand landed on my thigh. "Are you ready, Princess?"

I flashed a smile with a nod. "I am, Your Highness."

He looked down at the dashboard and at the center console. "Do you know how to drive this?" Before I could answer, he put the car in gear, and sending gravel flying, pulled away from the castle.

"Oh," I yelped as I reached for the door handle and the console.

"Relax. I was teasing."

There was something magical in seeing his smile and hearing the levity in his tone. It wasn't until we passed the first gate that he let out a breath. His grin was mesmerizing as he stared at the road ahead. A finger to his lips and I knew he didn't want me to speak.

Once past the final gate, Roman slowed the car to a stop.

"What?"

He shook his head.

For the next few minutes, Roman searched throughout the interior of the car and even in the boot. Once he was satisfied, he got back in the driver's seat, closed the door, and put the car in gear.

"Do you think they'd spy on us?" I asked.

"I know they would. I didn't give them enough notice of our departure." He sighed with a grin. "Let's enjoy our freedom if only for a few hours."

I laid my gloved hand on his arm. "It's stifling. You feel it?"

Roman nodded.

I went on, "That's what you told me before we were married. You also promised to make it not so."

"I didn't realize how much pressure there would be." He shrugged as we drove through the countryside, slowly going farther up the mountain. We passed homes with smoke curling from the chimneys. Small villages seemed quiet without the signs of upheaval. Patches of snow as well as melted areas showing the winter foliage alternated along the side of the road. "I honestly had no idea what I was in for."

"I warned you to go back."

His expression darkened. "In the journals I read last night, his outlook was bleak. I believe he wanted his time to end."

"Couldn't he simply say he quit?"

"No. You have more freedom in that than I or he. You could walk away citing irrevocable differences. I on the other hand...well, the heir can't just leave."

Laying my head against the seat, I sighed. "Unless they can bring back the real Roman."

"I'm not sure that's an option."

"I never knew." I shook my head. "If I'd have known..."

"Lord Martin is concerned about you."

"Me?" I asked.

"Yes, he fears you'll learn the truth, and that truth will put you in danger."

I recalled my discussion with Lady Buckingham, and my smile returned. "My mistress doesn't know about you. Today, she was timidly encouraging."

"Timidly encouraging?"

"She doesn't fully trust you or your more recent calmness."

"That's good."

"Why is that good? You're trustworthy."

"If she doesn't trust me," Roman said, "it means she still believes I'm Roman, the same man, a different attitude."

"She mentioned that I'm smiling more."

His dark gaze turned to me as his cheeks rose. "I love your smile. I told Lord Martin that I felt like I was taking you on a date."

"I dared to think the same." I looked out over the countryside. "Where are we going? Lady Buckingham brought me a light lunch, saying you had plans."

"Mount Reugen."

I tilted my head. "Why there?"

"I read about the beautiful view."

"But there are no restaurants. It's wilderness."

"That's why I asked the cook to pack us a picnic."

If I were to swear under oath how I felt at that exact second, I'd swear my heart fluttered. "A picnic in the snow?"

"My princess, I won't let you freeze."

Resting against the seat, I thought about our upcoming appearances. "Tomorrow we are scheduled to visit Odnessa. Wednesday is Forthwith. Isabella invited us to spend Tuesday night with them."

Roman's jaw clenched as he nodded.

"What's wrong?"

"I will accept their offer."

"You wouldn't agree to sleeping there."

"I must agree. I need to speak to Francis about Alek and Inessa."

"Was there anything in the journals that will help you?"

Roman shook his head. "Nothing, not one word about Inessa. Tonight, we'll check the phone and tablet. They should be fully charged."

"I don't want you to meet with her," I confessed. "I'm...I'm jealous."

Roman's hand came back to my thigh. "You have my heart. Don't question that."

I didn't want to question.

Yet life had delivered blows that were unforeseen.

Caught in the reflection of what was, I feared reality was too near.

White and silver clouds floated in the pale-blue sky as Roman drove us to the entrance of the preserve. In the summertime, the area would be filled with mountain climbers and swimmers. The last time I'd been here I'd yearned to paddleboard. Of course, that visit was official and instead of relaxing, I was present as a sparkling accessory. Even mentioning a recreational activity would have been met with discontent.

With winter around the corner, there wasn't another car or person in sight as we followed the narrow road. Roman parked the car and turned to me. "How about an adventure, my princess?"

Fastening the front of my coat and donning my leather gloves, I nodded. "I trust you, my prince."

Cool breezes swirled around as Roman opened my door and offered me his hand. His gloved fingers surrounded mine as I stepped onto the crunchy gravel. Together we followed a path upward to a crest. My eyes blurred and my cheeks prickled from the cold as we reached the summit.

Before us was a basin lake, partially ice covered, with tall snowcapped mountains on each side. Despite the breeze, the lake hidden in the valley was still, a mirror reflecting the mountains all around.

"This is beautiful," I said.

"Have you been here before?"

"Once, but it was for crown duties and warmer."

Roman looked down at our feet, seeing my leather boots. "I'm glad you decided to wear shoes."

I leaned against him as he surrounded me with his arm. The spicy aroma of his cologne lingered in the weave of his wool coat. He reached for my chin and lifted it until our lips touched.

"I was thinking," he said.

"About kissing me again? I like that idea."

Roman's smile shimmered in his dark eyes. "The blessing. I think we should have it done prior to the summit."

"So soon? Why?"

Roman exhaled, small crystals glistening in the air. "I anticipate there will be some sort of confrontation regarding Borinkia. It would be better if we publicly affirm our recommitment to our marriage before that happens."

"The summit begins on Friday." I was doing a mental countdown. "Thursday?"

Roman nodded. "Thursday."

"At Forthwith?"

"No, at Annabella. We'll invite the Duke and Duchess of Wilmington as well as the king and queen."

"The king and queen have only been to Annabella once since our wedding."

"Then this gathering will garner the news I need headed into the summit."

"Is that the only reason you want to do it?"

"No," he said, pulling me closer. "I want the whole fucking world to know that I'm committed to my wife, the most beautiful and amazing woman I've ever known."

"I feel none of this is fair to you." I thought about what Roman had said about the journals. "You could end up like Noah." I said his name quietly. "With a bleak outlook and feeling strapped down to me and Molave."

"Lucille, I've committed to Molave, but honestly, the country means nothing without you in it. My outlook isn't bleak. I have hope for what we can do together."

"Is King Theo as ruthless as Noah claimed?"

He shrugged, his shoulder moving. "I haven't figured that out. On the surface...King Theodore has replaced his own son at least twice to keep the monarchy headed the way he wants it to go. That in itself is ruthless. I might say he's resilient, unwilling to accept circumstances and refusing to accept that they're out of his control. He wants Molave and the Godfreys to succeed. Is that ruthless?"

"I don't know anymore."

"Come, let's see what the kitchen packed for our lunch."

The sun was near the horizon by the time we returned to Annabella Castle. Our passing the gates informed the guards we'd returned. As Roman drove us closer, Lady Buckingham, Lady Caroline, Lord Martin, and Geoffrey stood beside the exterior doors—our greeting party.

"Why do they do that?" Roman asked softly. "It's cold."

"Protocol." A smile lifted my cheeks. "And to be sure we returned."

"Maybe one day, we won't."

CHAPTER 31

Roman

Waiting for Lucille's arrival to my bedchamber was misery. Since Lord Martin left my suite, with each tick of the clock, I'd been positively itching to enter the secret room. I'd even approached the bookcase multiple times. The only thing that stopped me was remembering Lucille's request. I asked her to only open the room with me present, and she'd asked for the same.

Opening the secret door would be a minor offense but an offense all the same.

I wouldn't become Noah because I had the princess on my side. Despite how it looked to the world, our relationship was too new for me to betray her in any way, even simply opening the secret room.

Avoiding the temptation, I paced back and forth in my private parlor, praying for the door to open and her to enter. Finally, it happened.

Lucille's beautiful blue stare met mine before she smiled and curtsied. "Your Highness."

At the sight of her, relief sprinted through my circulation, instantly calming me. "My princess, I was about ready to go looking for you."

She came closer, the fresh scent of flowers surrounding her. "My mistress was full of questions about our drive. Bathing and dressing took longer than usual."

I brushed a rogue tendril of hair away from her face, tucking it behind her ear as my gaze lowered to her collarbone and soft flesh visible in the neckline of her dressing gown. "You're worth the wait."

Lucille swallowed.

Drawn by an invisible attraction, I lowered my lips to her neck, softly kissing behind her ear and downward. Her melodious noises filled my ears, fueling my desire. Taking a deep breath and smelling the concoction of bath salts and desire, I took a step back. "If I don't stop, we won't get any farther than the parlor."

"Here?"

"Oh, Princess, I would strip you down and take you on this rug." I looked around. "Or the sofa, table..."

Lucille's bare feet shuffled, and the rosy hue of her cheeks seeped down her neck.

Brushing my thumb over her cheek, I asked, "Does that sound desirable?"

With wide eyes, she nodded. "We've never..."

Fuck.

"Always in the bedchamber?" I asked.

"Always in the bed. Never..." Her hands came to her cheeks. "This conversation is...I'm embarrassed."

"Don't be." I reached for her hands. "I promise I'll take you in every room of our apartments."

She gasped. "Not in the connecting parlor."

"Oh, Princess, yes, on the table where they serve our meals."

Smiling, she shook her head. "Now, you're teasing me."

I lifted my brow. "I'm dead serious." And with the way the conversation had recirculated my blood, I was ready to do as I promised. "Fuck first or after we check the phone and tablet?"

"Your Highness?"

I reached for the sash of her dressing gown.

Lucille tugged her bottom lip as her blue orbs stayed fixed on me.

Pulling the tie free of its secured knot, Lucille's dressing gown gaped. My mouth grew dry, and my erection doubled in size. Running my fingertips from her neck down between her breasts and lower, I watched as her nipples tightened and the red of her areolas deepened. I couldn't hide my shock or arousal at this unexpected surprise. My gaze traveled beyond my touch, to her stomach and farther, to her freshly shaved mound. Lingering in a trance, I took in every sculptured curve and plane of her naked form.

My smile bloomed. "You forgot more than slippers."

"I waited until Mary left and then..." She shrugged.

Pulling the dressing robe from her shoulders, I let it drop, falling in a puddle at her feet.

"Where?" I asked.

Lucille turned right and then left. "I-I..."

I lifted her chin. "Are you wet?"

"You wouldn't—"

"Are you wet?" I repeated, my tone demanding an answer.

"Yes."

Taking her hand, I led her to the table. It wasn't as large as the one in the connecting parlor, but it was perfect for her introduction to a broader world of sexual pleasure. Without a word, I turned her around and pressed two fingers between her shoulder blades. A fast learner, Lucille complied, flattening her breasts on the tabletop and pushing her round ass toward me.

As I pulled myself from my pajama pants, I commanded, "Spread your legs."

Little by little she obeyed.

With each movement, she pushed up on her toes and her round ass tightened with anticipation.

One finger between her folds and I confirmed what she'd said. She hadn't been completely accurate. My princess wasn't wet—she was soaked. Leaning over her, I lowered my tone. "Hold on to the edge of the table. Otherwise, Lady Buckingham will find bruises on your hips."

"Your Highness." Her words were shaky as she complied. On each side of her, she wrapped her fingers around the table's edge.

Skirting my fingertips down her spine, I said, "You're absolutely stunning, and I'm painfully hard."

Craning her neck, she peered over her shoulder. In her gaze was the combination of expectancy mixed with trust. She didn't know me well enough to give the second to me, but I would take it and spend the rest of my life proving it wasn't ill placed.

"Seeing you like this," I confessed, "doesn't make me want to make love."

I saw the question forming in her expression.

"It makes me want to fuck you, hard. If it's too much, tell me to stop."

"No." Her smile shone as she nodded. "Do it. I want this."

Fisting my cock, I teased her folds, up and down. Each pass made me go from what was already hard to steel. Each pass covered my tip with her essence. No longer able to control myself, I plunged deep inside her. One strong thrust and I was buried in her tight pussy. Her core clamped down as the parlor filled with the sounds of her pleasure.

Being inside her was indescribable.

It was unfathomable the way she hugged me from within. I was on the verge of coming too soon. Hell no. Holding tight to her hips, I pulled out and pushed back. Faster and faster, I prodded, each time giving her all I had to give.

If this elation were a drug, I would be the addicted prince.

The slapping sounds our bodies made as they came together became our rhythm. While simultaneously, our incomprehensible noises created our melody. Lucille's alto whimpers and moans blended perfectly with my bass growls. Together, we were singing the song of princes and princesses before us. A song and dance repeated throughout the centuries.

Taking her as I was, I was a man possessed.

Not starved of food but of companionship.

I'd never had it.

I'd had sex.

But not this.

I'd never wanted a woman, to commit to a woman, to love and protect a woman like Lucille—ever. What was happening was more than sex. We'd done that many times. This was me staking my claim. If that sounded primitive, it was.

Since the dawn of time, mankind was created to be half of a whole, two people who were better together than apart.

It had taken me thirty-eight years and an upside-down crazy turn of events to find that other person. Now that I had her, I would never let her go.

I was lost in my building bliss when Lucille's body stiffened beneath me. Her fingers blanched as her grip tightened, and she called out. At nearly the same time, a roar rose from deep within my throat. My body trembled, quaking as I exploded. Wave after wave of pleasure washed through me as I came.

Panting for breath filled the parlor as I collapsed over her.

In the moments it took for us to regain our breath, I fell to the floor, bringing Lucille with me. Our union disconnected as she landed on my lap, and I cradled her in my arms. Her eyes glistened with unshed tears.

"I'm sorry if—"

Her finger came to my lips. "You're misinterpreting. I'm not sad. I'm happy. I've never felt so desired."

Looking down at her naked form, I asked, "Are you hurt...your hips?"

She closed her eyes as her smile grew. "I may not be

able to walk tomorrow, but that's not as important as how amazing that was." She lifted her lips to mine. After our kiss, she looked deep into my eyes. "This is real. Tell me if it isn't because I can't handle losing you again."

"This is fucking real, Lucille. It's a mess and a scandal waiting to happen, but it's real."

CHAPTER 32

Lucille

What I'd told Roman was the truth. Never had I felt as desired or wanted as I did in his parlor. What occurred was raw and real. My body was ablaze with explosions as nerve after nerve ignited. Even now, even after, muscles I didn't know existed made themselves known. In my reflection, it appeared as if I would need to explain my bruised hips. Despite my best efforts, Roman's unbridled passion left its mark.

As I emerged from the bathroom again covered by my dressing gown, my gaze met that of the prince.

The rumble of his voice and his sly grin twisted my core. "I think I mentioned I like you without clothes."

"The room is cold," I replied with a coy grin.

"I'm your prince."

His deep timbre reverberated through me, reminding me of receiving greater passion than I'd ever known. "Yes, Your Highness." I gave him a small curtsy.

In two or three long strides he was before me. "I'm quite sure that means you are supposed to obey me."

"Yes, Your Highness."

Lifting my chin with his thumb and forefinger, he brought my lips to his. When he stepped away, he handed me a pair of his socks.

Snickering, I took them. "Thank you."

"Or you could remain out here in the bedchamber. I'll go get the electronics and bring them out."

Picturing the narrow room with the unfinished walls, dust, and secrets caused me to shiver. "Yes, that would work."

Settling on the edge of his bed, I watched as he opened the secret room. Even from a distance, the cool air infiltrated his bedchamber. Roman disappeared a second before the room filled with light. Soon, he reappeared, tablet and phone in hand. "Are you ready to learn more?"

"I'd rather try for another previously unsullied surface."

"We didn't sully that table. We christened it."

"Oh, in that case, we could christen more."

"I like that idea, Princess." He laid the electronics on the bed at my side before reentering the room, turning off the light within, and closing the secret entrance.

Leaning back on my outstretched arms, I watched

as Roman came toward me. The uncertainty of what we may learn showed in the lines on his face and the rigidness of his jaw. "Are you worried?"

"I'm worried I won't learn what I need to know when I meet with Inessa."

"Don't meet with her."

He shook his head. "It's not that easy."

Sitting up, I reached for the phone and pushed the power button. The screen came to life with an indication for fingerprint identification. My eyes opened wide as I looked at Roman. "Fingerprint. The Firm didn't by chance change your fingerprints to his, did they?"

Roman's forehead furrowed. "No. Shit. Let me see." He reached for the phone and laid his finger over the sensor. "Unrecognized."

"If you do it again, it should give you the option to enter a pin."

Roman sat at my side, holding the phone so I too could see the screen. Nervously, I leaned against his bare shoulder. Closing my eyes, I inhaled his masculine scent. When I opened my eyes, there was now an option to enter a pin to unlock the screen.

He turned to me. "If we enter the wrong pin too many times, it will lock. Do you have any idea of what pin he would use?"

My mind spun. "If he were Roman, I'd say our

anniversary or the date we met, but he wasn't. I don't know what Noah would use."

"His birthdate?"

"Maybe. Do we know it?"

"I know Roman's," he said, speaking of the real prince.

Nodding, I said the date, "April fourteenth."

Roman entered the first four digits.

"Try again," he said with a sigh.

Standing, I paced back and forth. Seeing the bookcase, I said, "You said the titles were alphabetical. You said you notice detail. He wasn't about detail. He was compulsive. What about something simple like 1-2-3-4?"

"Too simple."

"You could try it," I suggested.

"If it's wrong, we've wasted a guess."

I pursed my lips.

"Fine." Roman entered the four digits. "Well, fuck. I guess he wasn't as complicated as I thought."

Hurrying to his side, I peered down at the phone. "Can you access email?"

"No, but there is a boatload of missed text messages."

Looking at the tablet, I asked, "Do you want me to look in the tablet while you read messages?"

"Do you think he locked it with the same pin?"

Shrugging, I said, "There's one way to find out." To our delight, the screen appeared, and the pin worked. "He had a secret email account." I pointed at the screen. "All of our email addresses are linked to the royal server. This isn't."

"Do you think he wanted this found?" Roman asked. "Wouldn't he use stricter pins or passcodes?"

"Maybe he knew he'd be replaced and wanted to help you."

"You're making him sound like a good man."

"He wasn't," I answered truthfully. "But maybe he wanted to make up for that?"

Roman stood and pulled back the blankets on his bed. "Come, join me."

"Yes, Your Highness," I said with a nod.

Soon, we were both sitting with our backs against the headboard, each reading from our individual electronic device. For only a moment, I looked over at the man at my side. "Is this how real people live?"

His dark gaze met mine. "What do you mean?"

"I don't know, this..." I looked at the list of emails and back up. "I don't mean learning secrets. I mean being comfortable and familiar with one another, enough so to read a book or check emails while lying in bed with one another?"

Roman's smile shone. "Yes, Princess. This is what

normal people do. They don't sleep in separate bedchambers."

"Maybe with time..."

He reached over and covered my hand with his. "Right now, I want to survive the summit. After that, your wish is my command."

Nodding, I swallowed the lump of emotions in my throat. In these stolen moments, I had my prince charming, the man of my dreams. When I was with Noah, I loathed our time together, and I wished for him to stay away. Now, my life was the exact opposite, a reflection. I didn't want this Roman to leave me, not for a day or a week.

With a sigh, I turned back to the emails.

"I don't know who most of these people are," I said, scanning over the senders' names.

Roman turned my direction. "Shit, Princess, look at this."

A chill ran over my flesh. "Is that from Alek Volkov? It's in English."

"The king told me that Roman—I—only mastered Norwegian and English."

"What does he say?" I asked.

Roman shook his head. "This goes back two months at least."

"Since you've been here."

He nodded as he read. "He's upset that I haven't responded."

"Should you?"

Exhaling, he laid his head back. "I think I should talk to Francis first."

"Do you trust him?" I gave my own question some thought. "I have never felt one way or the other about him. He's mostly quiet around me. He's good with the children."

Laying the phone on his lap, Roman reached for my hand. "I only trust you right now."

"Please be careful."

CHAPTER 33

Roman

Odnessa was a port city northwest of Annabella, in the Monovia province. Many of the shipping issues had come to a head in their ports. Earlier this morning, I'd been briefed that the backlog of shipping containers was being addressed. I'd also learned that the Ministry of the Interior was moving forward with Parliament on the program I'd talked about in Brynad. It was the appointment of representatives from each province to form a citizens' commission that would communicate with the ministry. Not only did it create a useful means of interaction, but it also gave the people a sense of power and control.

Our plan was to speak near the shipyard in Odnessa. My office in conjunction with the princess's arranged the site, coordinated with the royal guard and the territorial law enforcement, and made the formal announcement of our impending arrival.

After Odnessa, we were headed to Forthwith.

Reaching across the seat, I covered Lucille's hand with mine. "Don't be nervous."

Looking down, she nodded. "I'm not nervous about this."

"Forthwith?"

She lowered her voice. "My stomach is in knots. I fear I won't be able to spend time with Isabella and the children, knowing…" She exhaled.

Knowing I could be meeting with Inessa and possibly Alek Volkov.

"Thursday, we will be home. Cardinal Decoti will preside over our marriage blessing."

Her eyes opened wide. "You were able to schedule it?"

"Yes. The king said the queen would be excited. They will arrive on Thursday as well."

"Francis and Isabella?"

I shook my head. "I haven't mentioned it yet. Too many balls in the air."

Lucille nodded. "I wish my parents could be present."

How had I not thought of that?

"I'm sorry, I didn't even think…"

"No apologies," she whispered.

"We can delay."

The princess shook her head. "No, I will tell my mother during our next call. She'll be happy for us."

"Your Highnesses," the guard in the front seat said, turning toward us.

"Yes," I replied.

"According to the royal guards at the shipyard, the crowd is growing larger than expected."

"Is there a problem?" Lucille asked.

"No, ma'am. It's taking longer than anticipated to scan each person. They're bringing in more magnetometers."

"Scan?" Lucille asked. "No one in Brynad was scanned."

"It's for your safety," the guard replied. "The chief minister demanded it be done."

"What is she worried about?" Lucille asked me.

I hadn't been told of any direct threats. I squeezed her hand. "Just doing her job."

Blockades restricted traffic as we entered the city limits. Our caravan of vehicles was met by the territorial police, leading us toward the shipyards. Beyond our windows, the streets were lined with people. Some were waving the Molave flag. Others waved and called our names.

Both our driver and the second guard had earpieces with which they communicated with other guards on the ground. The same guard as before turned toward us. "They're recommending that you stay in the vehicle until more people can enter."

I looked down at my watch. "We said we'd speak at two p.m."

"Yes, sir. Odnessa's mayor will speak to the crowd and explain the delay."

Tugging at my collar, I took a deep breath.

This was part real and part pretend. My research had told me that Roman wasn't a fan of speaking to large crowds. In the recent past, doing so would make him uncomfortable and—surprise—irritable. Lord Martin had reminded me of that trait as he dressed me this morning. As our car progressed slowly along the route, we were visible to the people on the street.

One glance toward Lucille and it was difficult to stay stressed.

"Do you remember what we are to say?" I asked.

"Yes, Your Highness." She lowered her voice. "This is what I've dreamed of."

Her smile was breathtaking as she waved to the crowd. The slight downturn of her chin made her appear the perfect combination of timid and regal. I noticed signs beyond the window. Many read *Thank you, Princess and Prince*.

I smirked. "I see they give you top billing."

"I am but the moon to your sun."

Before I could respond, her hand landed on mine. "It is what you like me to say."

Well, that's bullshit, but so is most of this.

Our car came to a stop.

"Once the space is filled, we will speak."

The guard responded. "They won't all fit. We underestimated."

Lucille's lips curled.

This was exactly what she wanted, to show the crown and the ministry that together we could be spokespeople for the monarchy. The number of people present bolstered her argument.

"There will be other speeches," I replied.

Within the confines of the automobile, Lucille's and my communication was limited. Finally, we were given the sign to proceed. As the guard from the front seat opened his door, a thunderous roar came from the crowd. When Lucille's door was opened the air was filled with people chanting her name.

"Be sure there is a guard at her side," I said to the driver before scooting toward the open door. As I emerged, there were both cheers and jeers. Ignoring the jeers, I waved to the crowd. Following a step behind Lucille, I followed her up onto a temporary platform. My eyes scanned from side to side.

This was better than we'd been at the grocer's in Brynad. Here, we had space away from the crowd. Looking out over the sea of heads, I was equally aghast by the size of the gathering. The mayor was speaking and announcing our presence.

"Your Highness," she said, stepping away from the microphone.

Lucille stood dutifully at my side.

I took a step forward. "Good people of Molave."

More roaring cheers.

"I have much to thank you for and to tell you, but first, I believe you didn't come to see me but your princess."

The loudest cheers yet.

Lucille's gaze met mine as she smiled and curtsied. Next, she walked to the microphone. It took a full two minutes before the crowd quieted. I was transfixed as she addressed the people. Her care and concern were on full display. She spoke knowledgeably about the shipping issues, promising that we'd spoken with the king and promising that things would improve.

She spoke about the markets and filling the shelves.

Beyond the stage, the people were mesmerized by her presence, concern, and understanding of their problems. When one person yelled a question about obtaining health care, she was fully equipped to respond. As she bid the people adieu and she stepped back for me to take the microphone, the crowd responded with *We love you, Princess.*

Once the gathering quieted, I turned to Lucille. "They love you, and so do I."

An audible gasp came from the crowd followed by cheers.

I lifted my hand. "We're here to speak to you about your concerns. However, I feel it only fair to confess to you that I've made mistakes." The crowd grew silent. Every set of eyes was on me. "I regret some of the decisions I've made. I'm here to ask you to have faith in the monarchy. We aren't perfect, but we are trying." Clapping. "Some of my mistakes have been personal. To that account, we want you to know that in two days Senior Cardinal Decoti will be at Annabella Castle to offer new blessings on the princess's and my marriage." I reached back toward Lucille, who took my hand.

The cheering was nearly deafening.

"Our commitment is to you, the people of Molave, and to one another."

My speech went on to discuss the future commissions as well as more reassurance about the shipping, markets, and health care. As we waved to the crowd, I took Lucille's hand again and with guards on each side, we were led toward our car. Young children lined the path with flowers, each offering them to Lucille. By the time we entered the car, she held a bouquet bigger than Miss America's.

"You were fantastic," I whispered as our doors shut, and the guards entered the front seat.

"You told them about the blessing."

"I did."

"Was that approved?"

I scrunched my nose. "I'd call it improvisation."

She inhaled.

"Your Highnesses, it will be approximately a two-hour drive to Forthwith."

Leaning back, I unfastened my long wool coat and fastened my seatbelt. "I'd rather face that crowd again," I whispered.

"Me too," Lucille said.

CHAPTER 34

Lucille

Isabella greeted us as we entered, dressed in casual slacks and a soft jumper. Her dark hair was pulled back in a ponytail, and she appeared pleased to see us.

In all our years of marriage, this was only my third visit to Forthwith. The castle was beautiful, while the inside was strikingly modern. Isabella had a hand in the renovations. If she wasn't busy with her work as princess, duchess, and that of mother; interior design would be an alternate profession.

"Welcome," she said, offering Roman the customary 'Your Highness' and a curtsy.

He returned her greeting with a nod and something close to a huff. "Our apartments?" he asked the butler.

"This way, Your Highness."

Isabella reached for my hand. "Stay, let the grump go on ahead."

"I should—"

"You should tell me what's happening. I just received word of your speeches in Odnessa." Her dark eyes were open wide. "Come into the parlor."

I nodded to Lady Buckingham. "I'll be there shortly."

"Yes, Your Highness."

For only a moment, I stood and watched as Roman disappeared with the butler, followed by other Forthwith staff, Lady Buckingham, Lord Martin, and our luggage.

"Lucille," Isabella prompted.

"Where are the children?"

"Napping, I hope."

I unfastened the front of my coat as a maid appeared, taking it from me.

"Ma'am."

"Lady Nora," Isabella said, "bring us some warm tea. The princess has been traveling."

"Yes, ma'am."

Wrapping my arms around my midsection, I debated sitting or running. Yes, they were two completely alternate options. Until this moment, I hadn't realized that the last time I'd seen my sister-in-law was when she informed me of Roman's infidelity.

Isabella patted the sofa at her side. "We didn't get the chance to say goodbye when we left Molave Palace."

"I was a bit overwhelmed."

"I'm sorry I was the bearer of such horrible news."

Sitting down, I crossed my ankles beneath the sofa. "I think it's better that I know. We confronted things."

"How did he take it?"

Inhaling, I closed and opened my eyes. "There were words. This time they weren't only his. I said my piece."

"Good. I'd assume from the news from Odnessa, you are recommitting yourselves to one another?"

"Yes."

Lady Nora returned with a tray carrying a pot of tea and two cups. "Your Highnesses," she greeted as she placed the tray on the sofa table and poured hot tea into each cup.

"Thank you," Isabella said. "That will be all for now."

Lady Nora bowed her head and excused herself as she left us alone.

"I've been concerned about you," my sister-in-law said.

"Thank you for inviting us to spend the night. It would have been horrid driving back to Annabella and then turning around to come here."

She picked up one cup and saucer and handed it to me. Once she had her own, Isabella peered my direction. "Blessing. You'd said Roman had mentioned it before you knew..."

I inhaled. "He had. We've decided before the summit is best."

"We? Francis thinks it's more Roman."

"Why would Francis think that?"

Her lips came together. "I don't know what he thinks half the time. When I told him you'd mentioned a blessing, he laughed it off. When we were told about the speech, he seemed shocked and even angered."

I set the cup and saucer back on the table. "Isabella, do you know Inessa?"

She sat taller.

"Do you?"

"We've met."

My gaze narrowed. "And yet you didn't know about a relationship between her and Roman?"

"I didn't, Lucille. You must believe me." Isabella shrugged her shoulders. "Francis has maintained a relationship with the Volkovs. You see, in Wilmington, when he was younger, he and Alek knew one another."

"That's treason."

"No," she said. "Their relationship is not about Molave and Borinkia. They're...old friends."

"Alek and Inessa's father ran my mother's family from Letanonia."

"His father," she said placidly. "Not him. Not her.

Now that their father is growing old, Alek and Inessa want to bring Borinkia into the current century, just as you want to bring Molave."

"Molave's future is Roman's decision, not mine."

"He wants to have your marriage blessed." Her volume grew louder with each sentence. "He told a crowd that he loves you. You are the key to Molave's future. You can persuade him."

Turning my head, I scoffed. "When have you ever known me to persuade your brother?"

"I think that's what the Volkovs want, to work together with Molave for our joined future."

"Isabella, Molave will not join with Borinkia. My mother—"

"Sins of the fathers," she said, interrupting. "We are the future, not our parents."

Standing, I brushed the front of my slacks. "Isabella, thank you for your hospitality. I'm tired from our day. I hope you won't mind if I retire for a while. I want to be refreshed when the children wake."

"Lucille, don't be upset. The people of Molave listen to you. They were chanting that they love you. Don't you see, you can play a leading role in our future."

"That is my hope." I stood tall. "I shall return for dinner or before."

Isabella stood and reached for my hand. "Think about it."

"I shall think of nothing else."

By the time I made it up to the guest apartments, my stomach was doing full-out acrobatics. The sandwich I'd eaten before our speech was unsettled. Entering the connecting parlor, I hurried to my side of the apartments.

"Your Highness," Lady Buckingham said, standing as I rushed past.

I didn't slow as I made my way to the bathroom. Falling to my knees, I held my head over the lavatory as I gagged. My stomach twisted painfully as what remained of my lunch came back up. When there was no more to vomit, I laid my head on my arm over the seat. My forehead was slick with perspiration.

"Lucille?" Lady Buckingham questioned.

"Nerves," I replied. "Something Isabella said was unnerving."

"Here, ma'am."

I turned to see a glass of water in her grasp. Standing, I held to the wall as my knees felt unsteady.

"I can help you."

"No," I said, shaking my head. "I'm fine." Walking to the sink, I took the water, rinsed, and spit. I repeated the procedure a few times. The reflection staring back at me in the mirror was too pale. "I think I want to lie down." And then I remembered Roman, Francis, Inessa... I turned to my mistress. "Where is the prince?" I pushed past her. "I need to see him."

"He's gone. Lord Martin said something about a meeting."

My heart sank and ached at the thought.

A meeting.

With Inessa Volkov.

"Let me help you, Princess."

Fighting back tears, I nodded. "Thank you."

CHAPTER 35

Roman

"Where are we going?" I asked Francis as he drove us away from the castle.

He gave me a side glance. "This isn't working the way we planned." He pounded the heel of his hand on the steering wheel. "We were so fucking close."

"We can make a new plan," I said. "Now that I'm back at Annabella and even at the summit, I can contact Inessa."

"And tell her that you're rededicating yourself to Lucille?"

"It's a ploy," I lied. "You should have heard how the crowd ate it up."

Francis shook his head. "I didn't understand what happened at first."

"With?"

"With everything. How at one moment it's all working as planned and then it's fucked up...royally." He laughed.

Ahead of us down the road, a small cabin-like structure came into view.

The way the small hairs on the back of my neck stood to attention, I feared I'd made a mistake getting in Francis's car. Then again, I'm the prince. We're still on Forthwith grounds.

As Francis slowed, I noticed a small pond beyond the cabin.

"Do you remember this place?" he asked.

"Of course."

He nodded and shut off the engine.

As he got out of the car, I contemplated jumping into the driver's seat.

Francis leaned into the open door with a grin. "This is where I keep the good stuff, the cigars and bourbon your sister doesn't know I have."

Fuck.

Cigars and bourbon.

I opened the door to my side and stepped out into the frozen ground. The pond again caught my eye. However, despite the water being completely frozen and snow covered, a small square was cut away. "Ice fishing?" I asked.

At the same time, the door to the cabin opened.

I stopped as I stared at my own image.

"Noah?" I questioned.

"Oh," Francis said, "remember how I was

confused? You see, I was never told about Noah...about Noah not being Roman. Isabella still doesn't know."

Noah's dark stare was focused on me.

"Imagine my shock," Francis went on, "when I received a visitor, my brother-in-law. But my sister's brother was in Molave. I knew that. Fuck, I thought I was seeing double."

"You're alive," I said, stunned at the sight before me.

"You know my name. That means you found what I left behind."

I nodded. "I was afraid you were dead."

"I was supposed to be. Lord Avery got me to safety, not in time to save himself. The king was presented with two charred bodies."

I took a staggered step backward. "King Theodore called for your death?"

"Tell me you're smart enough to figure that out," Noah replied. "You've also fucked up my hard work. You see, Theo was supposed to be the one dead, not me. I would have been king."

"You're free now." I looked from Noah to Francis. "He's free. Help him get away."

Francis smiled. "We have a new plan." He nodded to Noah.

My heart stuttered as Noah pulled a pistol from his back waistband. "Whoa," I said, lifting my hands. "I took a damn job. If you want it back..." As the words came out, I knew I couldn't let this man back near Lucille.

He stepped closer, the gun raised. "Did they promise you riches? Did they tell you to bed the princess? I suppose you're supposed to get the whining cunt pregnant."

Standing tall, I clenched my jaw. "You're wrong about the princess."

His nostrils flared. "There can't be two of us."

I turned to my brother-in-law. "Do something."

"Whatever your name is," Francis said, speaking to me. "Let me share a bit of family history."

My gaze went to Noah and his gun. "Not a good time."

"This pond, it's where Theo and Anne's first son drowned. I thought it was an appropriate place for them to find their second son's body. Not that you're really their son."

"You can't be serious."

He nodded. "I could hand you a gun, too. Then the two of you shoot it out. With both of you gone, Isabella will rule."

"No, she won't," I said, hoping what I was about to say was true. "Lucille is pregnant. If that baby is a boy, he will rule."

"Fuck," Francis growled.

I turned to Noah. "Go. Leave. I won't tell anyone you're alive."

The gun wavered in his grasp. "I can't do this."

"Don't do this," I screamed.

The ground shook as the gun's blast echoed through the cold air and red spatter rained over the snow.

CHAPTER 36

Lucille

I woke from my nap with a start as I looked around the unfamiliar bedchamber.

"Roman," I called out.

The door opened inward as Lady Buckingham appeared. "He's still gone with the duke."

My stomach twisted as I wrapped my arm around my midsection. Lady Buckingham came closer. "Are you still not feeling well?" She laid her hand on my forehead. "You're not warm."

I tried to think back to the procedure. It had only been two weeks, but I could have gotten pregnant before that. Looking up at her concerned expression, I whispered, "Did we bring a pregnancy test?"

Her eyes opened wide. "Yes, but the king would want the royal physician—"

"Get me the test."

This wasn't the first time my mistress and I had stood over a small indicator stick. It was the first time the lines began to form as we waited the recommended three minutes. I reached for her hand, afraid my mind was playing tricks.

The result didn't take three minutes.

It hardly took any time at all for both lines to become visible.

I staggered backward to the wall. "It's positive." I looked up at Lady Buckingham. "It's positive."

She nodded as her smile grew. "You should rest."

"I need to tell Roman."

Thank you for reading RESILIENT REIGN. I hope you'll continue the story of the Prince and Princess of Molave in book three of Royal Reflections series, RAVISHING REIGN.

What to do now

LEND IT: Did you enjoy RESILIENT REIGN? Do you have a friend who'd enjoy RESILIENT REIGN? RESILIENT REIGN may be lent one time. Sharing is caring!

RECOMMEND IT: Do you have multiple friends who'd enjoy my dark romance with twists and turns and an all new sexy and infuriating anti-hero? Tell them about it! Call, text, post, tweet...your recommendation is the nicest gift you can give to an author!

REVIEW IT: Tell the world. Please go to the retailer where you purchased this book, as well as Goodreads, and write a review. Please share your thoughts about RESILIENT REIGN on:

*Amazon, RESILIENT REIGN Customer Reviews

*Barnes & Noble, RESILIENT REIGN, Customer Reviews

*Apple Books, RESILIENT REIGN Customer Reviews

* BookBub, RESILIENT REIGN Customer Reviews

*Goodreads.com/Aleatha Romig

ROYAL REFLECTIONS SERIES:

Riled Reign (prequel)

September 2022

RUTHLESS REIGN

November 2022

RESILIENT REIGN

January 2023

RAVISHING REIGN

April 2023

READY TO BINGE:

SIN SERIES:

Prequel: WHITE RIBBON

August 2021

RED SIN

October 2021

GREEN ENVY

January 2022

GOLD LUST

April 2022

BLACK KNIGHT

June 2022

STAND-ALONE ROMANTIC SUSPENSE:

SILVER LINING

October 2022

KINGDOM COME

November 2021

DEVIL'S SERIES (Duet):

Prequel: **"FATES DEMAND"**

Prequel - March 18

DEVIL'S DEAL

May 2021

ANGEL'S PROMISE

June 2021

WEB OF SIN:

SECRETS

October 2018

LIES

December 2018

PROMISES

January 2019

TANGLED WEB:

TWISTED

May 2019

OBSESSED

July 2019

BOUND

August 2019

WEB OF DESIRE:

SPARK

Jan. 14, 2020

FLAME

February 25, 2020

ASHES

April 7, 2020

DANGEROUS WEB:

Prequel: "Danger's First Kiss"

DUSK

November 2020

DARK

January 2021

DAWN

February 2021

* * *

THE INFIDELITY SERIES:

BETRAYAL

Book #1

October 2015

CUNNING

Book #2

January 2016

DECEPTION

Book #3

May 2016

ENTRAPMENT

Book #4

September 2016

FIDELITY

Book #5

January 2017

* * *

THE CONSEQUENCES SERIES:

CONSEQUENCES

(Book #1)

August 2011

TRUTH

(Book #2)

October 2012

CONVICTED

(Book #3)

October 2013

REVEALED

(Book #4)

Previously titled: Behind His Eyes Convicted: The Missing Years

June 2014

BEYOND THE CONSEQUENCES

(Book #5)

January 2015

RIPPLES (Consequences stand-alone)

October 2017

CONSEQUENCES COMPANION READS:

BEHIND HIS EYES-CONSEQUENCES

January 2014

BEHIND HIS EYES-TRUTH

March 2014

***

STAND ALONE MAFIA THRILLER:

PRICE OF HONOR

Available Now

***

STAND-ALONE ROMANTIC THRILLER:

ON THE EDGE

May 2022

***

THE LIGHT DUET:

Published through Thomas and Mercer Amazon exclusive

INTO THE LIGHT

June 2016

AWAY FROM THE DARK

October 2016

***

TALES FROM THE DARK SIDE SERIES:

INSIDIOUS

(All books in this series are stand-alone erotic thrillers)

Released October 2014

* * *

ALEATHA'S LIGHTER ONES:

PLUS ONE

Stand-alone fun, sexy romance

May 2017

ANOTHER ONE

Stand-alone fun, sexy romance

May 2018

ONE NIGHT

Stand-alone, sexy contemporary romance

September 2017

A SECRET ONE

April 2018

MY ALWAYS ONE

Stand-one, sexy friends to lovers contemporary romance

July 2021

QUINTESSENTIALLY

Stand-alone, small-town, second-chance, secret baby contemporary romance

July 2022

* * *

INDULGENCE SERIES:

UNEXPECTED

August 2018

UNCONVENTIONAL

January 2018

UNFORGETTABLE

October 2019

UNDENIABLE

August 2020

ABOUT THE AUTHOR

Aleatha Romig is a New York Times, Wall Street Journal, and USA Today bestselling author who lives in Indiana, USA. She has raised three children with her high school sweetheart and husband of over thirty years. Before she became a full-time author, she worked days as a dental hygienist and spent her nights writing. Now, when she's not imagining mind-blowing twists and turns, she likes to spend her time with her family and friends. Her other pastimes include reading and creating heroes/anti-heroes who haunt your dreams!

Aleatha impresses with her versatility in writing. She released her first novel, CONSEQUENCES, in August of 2011. CONSEQUENCES, a dark romance, became a bestselling series with five novels and two companions released from 2011 through 2015. The compelling and epic story of Anthony and Claire Rawlings has graced more than half a million e-readers. Her first stand-alone smart, sexy thriller INSIDIOUS was next. Then Aleatha released the five-novel INFIDELITY series, a romantic suspense saga, that took the reading world by storm, the final book landing on three of the top bestseller lists. She ventured into traditional publishing with Thomas and Mercer. Her books INTO THE LIGHT and AWAY FROM THE DARK were published through this mystery/thriller publisher in 2016.

In the spring of 2017, Aleatha again ventured into a different genre with her first fun and sexy stand-alone romantic comedy with the USA Today bestseller PLUS ONE. She continued the "Ones" series with additional standalones, ONE NIGHT, ANOTHER ONE, MY ALWAYS ONE, and QUINTESSENTIALLY THE ONE. If you like fun, sexy, novellas that make your heart pound, try her "Indulgence series" with UNCONVENTIONAL. UNEXPECTED, UNFORGETTABLE, and UNDENIABLE.

In 2018 Aleatha returned to her dark romance roots with SPARROW WEBS. And continued with the mafia romance DEVIL'S DUET, and most recently her SIN series.

You may find all Aleatha's titles on her website.

Aleatha is a "Published Author's Network" member of the Romance Writers of America and PEN America. She is represented by Kevan Lyon of Marsal Lyon Literary Agency and Dani Sanchez with Wildfire Marketing.

facebook.com/aleatharomig
twitter.com/aleatharomig
instagram.com/aleatharomig

Made in the USA
Columbia, SC
27 January 2023